Make Mine The Italian

A **Millicent Winthrop** Novel: Book 2

by

Gwen Overland

writing as

NINE WAVES MEDIA

Make Mine the Italian:
A Millicent Winthrop Novel: Book 2

Copyright © 2023 Gwen Overland

Cover Art by Rhian Awni

Book Design and Formatting by Anthony Boyd

Published in the United States by Nine Waves Media
More info at NineWavesMedia.com

ISBN: 978-1-959588-01-6

Acknowledgments

To my trusted writer friend, Cynthia Rogan, thank you for taking the time to read my work and for providing valuable feedback.

And to Marisa Brown at Venus Promotions for her constant attention to the marketing of myself and my books.

To my formatter and publisher at Nine Waves Media, Anthony Boyd and editor Rebecca Scott. These four people have been invaluable to me as I've journeyed through the writing of this series.

A huge thanks to Rhian Awni for my extraordinary, playful cover art.

And as always, a huge thanks to my devoted family, who never seem to mind the hours I spend away from them doing what I love second to them.

And a special thanks to my late maternal grandmother, whose name I've lovingly appropriated as my pseudonym.

Chapter 1

Nürnberg, Germany

The Grundig-Stadion, Nürnberg's soccer stadium, was bathed in the bright crisp sunshine of an October afternoon. Emotions rode high as they always did whenever Stuttgart came to town. This team was one of Nürnberg's most competitive rivals.

Thirty three minutes into the game against Stuttgart and Riccardo Stillitano, well known mid-fielder for FC Nürnberg, was motioned by the assistant coach to come in. The sub, a new kid from the Ivory Coast, waited anxiously for Riccardo to make it to the sideline before he too ran in to take his place.

What was the problem? Riccardo wondered. Nürnberg had struggled in the last game with Stuttgart, but today things were going far better, and mostly due to his own efforts. He felt particularly strong that day, so why was he being called off?

"Stillitano, you gotta phone call, mate. I think it's your dah. Somethin' about your mum," yelled Birmingham Billy, a benched forward on the team. He was always full of pranks and practical jokes, but today he wasn't fooling around, Riccardo could see it in his eyes.

"Grazie, amico," Riccardo returned.

Mamma? Is she all right? What was wrong? Papa would never call during a game unless it was an emergency. She always had problems with the breathing, but as of her last phone call with him, everything had been fine. Perhaps she fell.

He told papa a year ago to replace the loose stones in the garden walkway, but so far he hadn't.

Had mamma tripped and fallen?

Riccardo, noticeably shaken, grabbed his warm ups and water bottle from off the dugout bench and ran into the club house changing room. His heart pounded within his chest as he made his way down the stadium hallway toward the locker room. Tears welled up in his eyes as he reached for the handle of the door.

No sooner had he entered the room, the sweet, sickening smell of chloroform filled his nostrils as two strong arms came at him from behind, one wrapping itself around his neck, the other pressing a cloth to his face.

Not a word was said by either him or his assailant as Riccardo drifted into darkness.

***

Bad Reichenhall, Germany

"Mmmmm. Oh . . . ."

The diminutive, face-down figure of a half naked woman moaned from the narrow massage bed beneath her. It'd been far too long since the woman had been in such a compromised position, and she wasn't going to move an inch until the gentleman above her had his way. Thus, the firm but gentle hands of Helmut worked their way up Millicent Winthrop's knotted and aching spine.

"Again, please. Don't stop."

Millicent knew she should be embarrassed to make such an uninhibited vocal display of her relaxed pleasure, but, by God, she paid dearly for this treatment, and she wasn't going to cheapen her experience by withholding herself from enjoying it.

Now the dexterous hands moved to iron out the contorted muscles of her hamstrings. Helmut's warm palms pressed into the back of her left leg and smoothed out the tightly pretzeled muscles as he pulled each hand away from the other in opposite directions.

"Yes, yes, oh, yes."

It occurred to Millicent at that very moment that should someone outside the privacy of Helmut's therapy room hear her wails and groans, they may mistake her undeniable pleasure for something quite different from what it truly was. She began to giggle at the thought.

"Tee-hee-hee."

"Is Fräulein ticklish?" asked Helmut concerned.

"Oh, no. Tickled, perhaps, but not ticklish. Thank you, dear Helmut, for asking."

Millicent sighed. The last four months had been brutal. Not only had her latest crime-solving adventure proved less than reputable, but she seemed to be going absolutely nowhere with Dr. Alfredo Martolini, her psychiatrist, under whose care she'd been for the last two and a half years. You see, Millicent suffered from memory loss and not of the short term variety.

She absolutely couldn't recall a single thing about herself nor her life prior to an airlift from America three years earlier. One which left her deposited at the well-reputed Maudsley Hospital in South London, where she'd met for the first time the handsome Italian doctor.

That much she did remember and no wonder. Alfredo was what one would describe as *easy on the eyes*. Simply thinking about him forced another long sigh from out of her muscle-mashed body.

"Madame seems to be enjoying her massage today?" Helmut asked in his heavily accented baritone voice. The German's skilled fingers rubbed her scalp from near her ears up to the top of her head.

"*Danke sehr*, Helmut. Thanks to you I feel extraordinary." Millicent knew to thank Helmut as often as possible, as he was one of the best masseuses in the world. And the last thing she wanted to do was lose his favor.

Suddenly a light rap was heard at the door. "Fraulein Winthrop," announced a young woman's voice from outside the door. "Someone's on the phone demanding to talk to you. He won't allow me to take a message. Do you wish to take this call? Or should I tell him to, as you say, get lost?"

"Oh dear. Did he by any chance identify himself?" Millicent inquired.

"Ja. I believe he said his name was Herr Smythe," the girl answered.

"Oh, yes, by all means. Please tell *Mr.* Smythe I'll be with him in a quick moment."

With that Millicent reluctantly removed herself from the massage table, wiggled herself into the white terry robe draped over the chair, excused herself from Helmut's ever-attending presence, and took the phone with her into a nearby private room. After making sure she was alone and the door securely closed, Millicent spoke as quietly as possible into the phone.

"Hello? Millicent Winthrop here," she said timidly.

"Millicent, it's good to hear your voice. You sound quite relaxed. Much more so than the last time I spoke with you."

Make Mine The Italian

You would, too, if you had a series of multiples on the therapy table.

"Oh, yes, I feel . . . uh . . . indescribably refreshed. Thank you for noticing," she quipped.

Mr. Smythe always spoke to Millicent with the tenderness and care of an elder statesman. Yet at the same time with impeccable pronunciation, salted-and-peppered with the precise elocution of an English lord. And well he should, after all, he was Sir Buckminster Smythe, retired detective of Britain's own Scotland Yard.

"It indeed took me some days to find you this time, dear Millicent. I finally traced you back to Bad Reichenhall. You know, I believe you're forming some inestimably expensive habits, Millicent dear," he teased.

How well she knew. Millicent rarely spent a penny unless it was on a seven course gourmet meal from one of the most expensive restaurants in the world, or in attendance at a professional game of men's soccer. Portsmouth FC, formerly of the English Premier League and now in the Championship League was her team.

Or merely relaxing for a two-to-three day respite in one of the most luxurious first-class health and beauty spas in the world. Bad Reichenhall was her favorite.

"Now Bucky, you know what's stipulated in my contract." Millicent teased in return. "Besides, lately I've been feeling overwhelmingly fatigued and frustrated with myself."

Mr. Smythe immediately noticed her tone turn serious.

"Oh, Millicent, please don't feel badly about our last endeavor. At least you found where the young man had been detained, which was so much more informative than anything Interpol or Scotland Yard came up with.

"And ultimately we were able to save his life. I do deeply apologize we weren't, however, able to move as quickly as we needed in order to catch the kidnapper or retrieve the ransom money."

"And I'm so sorry I wasn't able to solve the crime before putting that young Spanish goalkeeper's life in danger." She was more than sorry, she was mortified.

How he must've suffered.

"Millicent, dear, I've been in this business of apprehending criminals for some forty years now, and I haven't had a perfect record by any means. You're new to this field and must realize not every case is going to be happily solved.

"One does one's best. That's all we can realistically do as we aren't perfect ourselves. Nor have we the same diabolical mind set as every monster in this dangerous world of ours."

"I know that, but . . . I only wish . . . well . . . you know."

"Yes, Millicent, I do. In the meantime, you must give yourself permission to indulge. With cases as difficult as this last one, you and I must be fully ready to move forward when called upon."

"Yes sir. I'll give it my best, sir."

Mr. Smythe couldn't help but hear the frustrated sadness in Millicent's voice. For that was all Millicent had been *trying* to do since her tragic accident three years ago. When during a California earthquake a ceiling tile dislodged, careened down upon her head, and embedded itself into the left side of her scalp. About two inches into her black-brown hairline, to be exact.

Since that event, Millicent had forgotten everything about her past life, and still from time to time had difficulty remembering current events, people's names, or who she truly was. In fact, her earliest memory was waking up and looking into the dreamy brown Italianate eyes of one Dr. Alfredo Martolini, psychiatric intern at Maudsley Hospital of South London, a facility dedicated to his life-long passion, the study of amnesiac disorders.

She let out a third long sigh.

"Aaaaaahhhhh!"

"Millicent, I know it's only been a few weeks, but I'm afraid we've another problem here at FIFA. Are you ready to take on yet another case?"

FIFA, short for the Fédération Internationale de Football Association, was the governing body of international football and headquartered in Zurich, Switzerland. Mr. Smythe was FIFA's chief of security and had some time ago while reading a research article by Dr. Martolini," The

Connection between Amnesia and the Diabolical Thinking Patterns of the Criminal Mind", learned of Millicent's uncanny ability to solve the most difficult of criminal puzzlements.

Apparently Alfredo Martolini noticed this connection with several of his patients, but none with so great a skill as that of a Miss Millicent Winthrop.

Millicent had only one previous assignment as a sleuth with FIFA. As a matter of fact, she basically had only one crime solved to her credit, FIFA or no FIFA. Although unaware as to how or why she was so good at her craft, Millicent knew she had some talent.

During the past two years she'd been brought in as a consultant for one interesting crime after another. Embezzlement, fixed betting, referees on the take, merely to name a few. Yet never kidnapping, and certainly not attempted murder. That was, not until her last case.

"Why, yes, of course I'm ready. I feel fully refreshed and can meet you at FIFA headquarters tomorrow. First, however, I must fulfill my appointment with Dr. Martolini. You understand." Although Millicent's words rang confidently professional, both she and Bucky couldn't help but notice how her breathy voice shook ever so slightly.

"Now, don't push yourself, Millicent. True, we need to move on this new case, and soon, but we can certainly work with someone else if need be. Perhaps with more time you will be more yourself."

Millicent snorted.

"Yes, well, I believe there's something of a saying which speaks about getting back on the horse, correct? Honestly, Bucky, I'm as ready as I'm ever going to be, at least until I get my full memory back. I will pack this evening, take a late morning flight to Venice, and be in Zurich no later than tomorrow afternoon."

"All right, Millicent. As usual, one of our jets will be at your disposal and will pick you up in the morning. Sleep well and have a safe trip, dear. Until tomorrow."

Mr. Smythe reluctantly hung up the phone. He knew Millicent needed more rest, but time was scarce with very little to spare. Another footballer had gone missing, and this time without a ransom note or a single clue left behind.

***

Zurich, Switzerland

Chief Inspector Buckminster Smythe didn't know why he worried so much about Millicent. Certainly it wasn't because she was inept or even because she was a woman. Over the years he'd overseen plenty of capable women agents, but none of whom he cared for in such a fatherly manner.

He and his wife of some twenty-five years had never had the privilege of having children, which is just as well in some ways since his job didn't allow for him the usual eight to five, Monday through Friday, kind of hourly schedule.

Yet he still carried a special place in his heart for Millicent, as did his wife Sabrina.

Perhaps it was because in some ways Millicent *was* so very incapable. She dressed like an eccentric, acted as naïve as a schoolgirl, and yet had the strategic thought patterns of a heinous criminal.

On top of that, she had an uncanny ability for getting desperately lost. If it wasn't for Holmes and Watson, her two short thick-set pugs, Millicent would never find her way anywhere and back—and then not until she wandered about for hours trying to remember where she'd been. Still, Millicent was special in her own way, and that way was what Bucky counted on to solve this new and challenging crime before him.

He punched the intercom button on his office phone.

"Madeline, please reserve the large conference room for an all security staff meeting tomorrow at four PM. Make sure everyone attends. No excuses. This is a Code Red alert. Do you understand? Code Red!"

"Of course, sir. Millicent isn't by any chance attending as well, is she?" Her tone of voice spoke of her disapproval.

Mr. Smythe paused.

"Do you have a problem with what I'm asking, Madeline?"

Mr. Smythe could hear a deep sigh at the other end of the intercom.

"Of course not, sir. It's as good as done."

Make Mine The Italian

Most of the Security Council had serious doubts about Millicent's abilities. Much of that was because they weren't privy to her background story or her previous dealings with Scotland Yard before being placed on contract by FIFA. In their opinion she was too inexperienced, too inconsistent, and far too strange in her speech, mannerisms, and dress to be taken seriously.

True, Millicent was new to detective work, but she did have more good days than bad. And her speech did sound a bit like an over-enunciating Shakespearean actor from yesteryear. She was always talking to herself, tripping over things.

On top of that her costume was reminiscent of that worn by Joan Hickson in the Agatha Christie *Miss Marple* television series. A longish tweed wool skirt, a undersized fitted jacket, a slightly damaged straw hat with a flower blooming out of the top, brown British walker shoes with a slight heel, beige colored tights bunched at the ankles, and spectacles with lenses the thickness of beer bottle bottoms clouded her clear blue eyes. Actually, she appeared to be more like a cross between Mary Poppins and Mr. Magoo.

Yet Mr. Smythe had a strong feeling in his gut that Millicent Winthrop was possibly the best and only answer to solving the current conundrum before him. If he couldn't change the attitudes of his colleagues regarding Millicent, then he could at least make sure they supported her detective work one hundred per cent.

"And get me Dr. Martolini on the line. If he doesn't answer, leave a message informing him I need to speak with him ASAP. Leave him my private number in case I'm not in the office when he calls. Got that?"

"I'll get right on it, sir," Madeline responded. "Dr. Alfredo Martolini."

"Thank you, Madeline. I know I don't have to tell you that time is of the essence."

The intercom went dead as Madeline efficiently followed her orders to the letter. She wasn't the most cheery person, but she always did her job well and with speed.

Mr. Smythe chuckled to himself. Millicent was most definitely an odd duck in these waters. No denying that. To say that the security staff at FIFA was a group of stuffed shirts put it mildly. Narrow-minded, grim-faced, skeptical, and without wit or imagination were attributes much closer to the truth. Yet that was why they so heavily relied on Millicent's perception of things. She had the curiosity of a child, true, but also the forensic skills of a genius.

Suddenly his thoughts were interrupted by Madeline's piercing voice on the intercom.

"Signor Martolini's on the line for you sir."

"Thank you Madeline. Please hold all other calls until I notify you."

"Of course, sir," she clipped. Within seconds the phone in Mr.

Smythe's office rang.

"*Buon pomeriggio, Alfredo,*" he answered. "*Come sta?*"

Chapter 2

Venice, Italy

Each week when Millicent arrived in Venice she stayed with her traveling companion Kathryn—affectionately known as Aunt Kate. Because they were no small troupe, what with the two dogs, their accompanying paraphernalia of plastic bones, pull toys, and assorted treats, and, of course, enough suitcases and garment bags to keep the bellhop busy for a good half hour.

The retinue usually stayed in their favorite junior suite at the Hotel al Ponte Antico, with a terraced view of the Rialto Bridge on the Grand Canal. Millicent's flight from Munich landed somewhat later than normal this particular day, so it wasn't until sometime after the noon hour before Millicent began the twenty minute trek from her hotel room to Dr. Alfredo

Martolini's office. The sun warmed the city in the clean freshness of an early afternoon in fall.

Millicent felt her heart race as she strolled along the canal walkways of Venice with her ever-loyal pugs, Holmes and Watson. These anxiety attacks were all too familiar occurrences for her. And since choosing her new career path as a sleuth, they had actually grown worse. It also didn't help her arrhythmia to know within minutes Millicent would once again be in a room alone with Dr. Alfredo Martolini, her handsome and sexy psychiatrist.

"I say, Millicent love," came a voice from somewhere near her feet, "why all the fuss?"

"Yeah," echoed another voice, thinner and higher, "why all the fuss?"

Millicent knew it was highly unusual for the canine species to speak at all, let alone with British accents, but Holmes and Watson were extraordinarily special pugs. And smart, too.

"I'm not sure exactly," Millicent answered in a muted whisper. It was one thing to hear voices. It was quite another to answer then. Especially if someone was close enough to hear.

Holmes, the alpha of the two, continued. "Your behavior today is highly unusual, Millicent love. Most of the time you're bright and cheery and all that sweet Pollyanna-like rubbish and dribble."

Watson, not to be left out, retorted, "Yeah, rubbish and dribble."

Millicent smiled lovingly at the two odd-looking dogs and decided then and there to put her dear friends' worries to rest.

"It's probably nothing. Merely nerves I guess. You know how I can get."

Holmes and Watson had been her beloved companions during the three lonely years of her treatment and subsequent release from the hospital in London. Litter-mates, they'd been given to her as therapy dogs while at the Maudsley Hospital fresh after her arrival.

Holmes's coat was faun-colored, silvery beige with dark markings on his four paws, tail, and face. Millicent always dressed him in a green sweater she'd knitted herself with a matching plaid tam to compliment his broad barreled chest and dignified face.

Except for his white muzzle, Watson was pure black and the runt of the two. Unlike Holmes, Watson was much more energetic and playful, never looking for trouble but somehow always finding it. Millicent dressed him in a short tuxedo jacket with tails and a white bow tie, hoping against all odds she could somehow dignify his mischievous personality.

Holmes cleared his throat and spoke with an eloquent British accent. "You should know more than anyone else, Millicent love, you have nothing to be nervous about. Dr. Martolini is a fine psychiatrist. And little by little you're making headway in your treatment. You may still not know exactly who you were, but you certainly know by now who you are."

Millicent and the two pugs stopped for a brief moment. She then stared down into Holmes's deep brown eyes. "I know. You're right. I wish the whole thing would move faster, that's all. It's been three bloody years and lately I feel more confused than ever."

Millicent would've given anything if what Holmes had said was true. She constantly worked at getting to know herself all over again, but even so there were still enormous gaps in her memory. For Millicent the passing of time felt like a constant daydream, flowing interchangeably between a strange fantasy world and reality.

"Perhaps it isn't in the cards for me to ever regain my silly little memory, whatever it may be worth."

Suddenly Watson peered up from his sniffing place and quipped, "Wha'ever it may be worth."

The three of them continued to walk up and down the canalways and over the many diminutive bridges which tie together the one hundred and four islands which make up the city of Venice. At last they were in the Dorsoduro, a quiet section of Venice, where stood the office and home of Dr. Martolini.

A fifteenth-century palace, the building had been in Alfredo's family since its origins. Suddenly it occurred to Millicent that by stepping back in time when entering this building she may find a way to step back into the inner reaches of her own subconscious mind and discover the truth of who she was.

The interior was breathtaking. The floors were inlaid with red and green marble and were spotless. To the right was a spacious room with a high filigreed ceiling of flowers and cupids held up by at least eight thick brown and grey perfectly rounded and polished marble columns.

To the left stood double carved wooden doors, which led to a room which Millicent could only assume was the old kitchen. Dead ahead, however, was the *pièce de résistance*—a dark brown and red marble staircase, minimally carpeted, with a landing some twelve steps up and then splitting into two curving stairways up to the second floor where Dr. Martolini's office waited for her arrival.

She was well aware the doctor also lived on this floor and that his mother lived an additional floor up. Although she'd never met Signora Martolini, it didn't stop her from imagining her frail and aging beauty and grace, not unlike one of the much younger portraits of her hanging on the walls of the lower level ballroom.

"Come, gentlemen. It's time for us to tempt fate as we ascend these lovely stairs. *La forza del destino.*"

Millicent loved to climb the luxurious steps each time she came to this lovely palatial home. Holmes and Watson scampered up to the first landing, and as they did, Millicent heard Watson quietly ask Holmes, "What are those delectable treats called again which the good doctor 'as waiting for us?" Watson drooled.

"Amaretto biscotti," Holmes panted.

"Oh, yeah," Watson snorted in his usual Cockney flavored inflection, *"La forza del Biscotti!"*

At the landing each dog ran up an opposite staircase, forcing Millicent's arms to stretch out at her sides. She had no recourse but to pull on each of their leashes with some strength in order to stop them. Holmes and Watson each fell down their respective staircase to the landing where Millicent stood. Then once up on their feet they rushed past her to once again charge up opposite staircases.

This is ridiculous.

The leash, now tangled around Millicent's feet, forced her to lose her balance and within seconds down she went. Flat on her back.

Dr. Martolini, hearing the mad barking of two overzealous pugs, came out of his office and leaned his head over the top railing.

"Buon giorno, Signorina Millicent. Do you by chance require assistance?"

Millicent lay on the floor—her glasses askew, her hat crumpled beneath her dislodged bun. Holmes and Watson, penitent as they were, began to lick her face in absolution.

Millicent could only look up into those deep brown eyes of the handsome doctor. Already frazzled from having to deal with the Keystone

Kop antics of her two dogs, Millicent momentarily got lost in the gaze of the man of her dreams.

"Oh, dear. I already feel as if I'm such an immense bother," she said, trying to sit up. "I wasn't going to bring the two of them this time, but they put up such a fuss, I couldn't ignore their protestations. And now not one of the three of us can make up our minds which staircase to choose."

Millicent realized she was rattling away—far too chatty for her own good—but there was nothing else to be done. Chaos is what she brought with her in one degree or another each time she met with Dr. Martolini. That and two flushed cheeks, a sweaty brow, and a medium-sized, slightly scrunched hat sitting on the top of her head.

As she sat completely up and re-adjusted her fogged up spectacles, Dr. Martolini elegantly descended the stairs, bent over to pick up the two errant leashes, and offered Millicent his hand.

"Here, signorina. Let me help you." And with that the doctor lifted Millicent to her feet and handed her the lead to Holmes while he took Watson's.

"Sedetevi, i miei due carlini." Immediately the two pugs responded to Dr. Martolini's firm but warm voice by sitting perfectly still, while Millicent gathered herself and made a few minor adjustments to her person. Holmes and Watson thought the world of the kind doctor and often told Millicent to that effect whenever she threatened to leave his care, which was usually

once a week directly after her session with him.

By the time they reached the doctor's office doorway, Holmes and Watson were unleashed and heading full speed ahead to their corner pillow where Dr. Martolini had already placed several slightly crumbled macaroons for their enjoyment.

"Nyum, nyum, nyum," Watson articulated. "These are my absolute favorite."

"Watson, do not speak with your mouth full. And stop that disgusting smacking of your jowls." Holmes had to keep a firm hand on Watson or entropy would undoubtedly follow.

"I say, you're deliberately munching far more than your share, 'olmes. You realize I get two cookies for every one you eat." Watson annihilated the macaroons faster than a Maserati at the Monaco Grand Prix.

"Dear God, why do I even try?" Holmes lifted his head up to the ceiling, snorted, and then shook his head, leaving Watson to finish licking up the few remaining crumbs. He made his way to the pillow, circled three times, and then plopped himself down.

Millicent couldn't help but giggle at the comical twosome as she gingerly stretched out on the soft Italian leather chaise lounge which awaited her. It directly faced the slender tapestried side chair Dr. Martolini always sat in for their weekly visits.

Millicent felt small enough in the presence of the astute *dottore* without also feeling swallowed up by the chubby cushions of his overstuffed divan. Dr. Martolini oddly stared at her, not exactly clear as to why she was chortling. Yet he was gradually getting used to these odd and sudden outbursts from Millicent and had learned over time to merely go along with whatever fantasy she was experiencing in a given moment.

"Signorina, I understand you're on another assignment. Sì?"

"Huh? Oh, yes. Yes, another assignment. That's what I wanted to speak to you about today. I'm not sure if I should continue with this avenue of employment any longer. I feel perhaps it's perhaps not for me after all."

"And why's that, signorina?"

"Well, uh, the truth is, um, I'm still having trouble with my memory. Obviously, I may always be unable to remember those things about myself prior to our meeting. But lately I'm also having issues with remembering what it is I need to do to garner results in solving these horrendous crimes. And if I can't remember that, then how can I continue to be of any assistance to anyone let alone FIFA in the future?"

"Surely you must remember your latest success?" Dr. Martolini coaxed.

"Well, I do and I don't. Truly, Doctor, I can't recall the full goings on of this latest affair with any measure of assurance. It's as if the film of my memory has had numerous clips edited out. And those clips are still missing, no matter how hard I try to edit them back in." Her voice shook as she struggled futilely not to weep.

Alfredo Martolini presented Millicent the clean, white handkerchief from his back pocket. He knew Millicent was anxious but felt that her problems didn't stem so much from her memory loss as they did from her lack of self-confidence.

"Signorina Millicent, please don't cry," he said, trying to comfort her as best he could. "We will continue to work at recovering your past, and when we do, then I'm sure you will be able to remember even these current, as you say, 'missing clips' from your memory. In the meantime, you must be strong and confident in yourself and your ability to solve even the most challenging of cases. Your talents, my dear Millicent, far outreach the difficulties of your mind."

He smiled at Millicent, and in that brief moment she believed him hook, line, and sinker.

***

Later that afternoon Alfredo Martolini went over in his mind the conversation he'd had with Millicent earlier in the day. He'd been alerted to her current fragile mental state by Mr. Smythe, a man whom he'd become close to since the publication of his research paper regarding Millicent's special talents.

Alfredo understood why FIFA had such an interest in Millicent. She was clever, bright, and had unusual thought patterns which were without saying outside of the box. It was also clear she could be of great service to FIFA and possibly to the world.

What had him most concerned, however, was how all of this was affecting Millicent. In spite of all her capable attributes, she was also fragile, childlike, shaken by her amnesia as well as her last case failure, and enormously confused.

Alfredo knew he shouldn't be annoyed by Mr. Smythe's demands on Millicent, but he couldn't help it. He felt as if she needed his protection and care, for Alfredo's only agenda was for Millicent's safety, happiness, and well-being. After all, he was her psychiatrist.

Funny, though, how out of all his clients, Millicent was the one special patient who took up most of his thinking. And it wasn't only because he was her doctor.

Millicent was charming—sweet in a kind of innocent and refreshing way, unlike most of the women he'd been seen with over the years. Alfredo's tastes ran more toward the sophisticated, long-legged, full-figured girls of his hometown, Venice. Think of the Mona Lisa and one has a pretty good idea as to his *donna perfetta*.

Millicent, on the other hand, was like a lost child, petite, and who knew what her figure was truly like under her loose, matronly attire. He wasn't even sure of her age. Maybe 40, or perhaps even 25.

Yet something about the cute way her nose turned up and her blue eyes twinkled whenever she spoke to Holmes and Watson made him curious and unsure of his own abilities of perception. And those glasses—*oh caro Dio in cielo!* Could she look any more ridiculous if she fastened binoculars to her face?

Enough! Sufficiente! He told himself as he felt his heart skip a beat. No way would he allow himself romantic inclinations toward Millicent. First of all, it was unethical—she was after all his patient.

And second—well, there actually was no second. Alfredo scanned over his notes in Millicent's file and told himself that in order to play it safe he needed to be careful, even though his heart told him he was heading toward a whole heap of trouble.

Chapter 3

Venice, Italy to Zurich, Switzerland

Millicent left for Zurich immediately after returning Holmes and Watson back into the care of Aunt Kate at the Hotel al Ponte Antico. She hoped once again she wasn't imposing on her friend, but this meeting at FIFA shouldn't take more than a few hours at best.

Millicent heard the water from the shower beating on the wall of the stall.

"Aunt Kate, I'm flying to Zurich on business, but I shouldn't be home too late."

No answer.

"Fiddle-sticks," she murmured under her breath.

She hated to leave a note, but she had no other choice. Clearly Aunt

Kate was unable to hear anything under the steady avalanche of warm spray from *la doccia*. Millicent nonetheless left Holmes and Watson enough water to last until her return, as well as two pint-sized bowls of food.

"There you are, gentlemen. Be good boys for Aunt Kate," she ordered,"and don't make a mess while I'm gone."

The two pugs glanced first at each other in bewilderment, then at Millicent.

"What the—"began Watson, but Holmes interrupted with a cordial, "Yes, Miss." And the two proceeded immediately to devour their afternoon ration of dog food as Millicent closed the door.

The flight took exactly sixty-five minutes. As soon as she deported the plane, a black sedan with tinted windows whisked her away to the spacious grounds of FIFA headquarters. The parking lot stretched itself around the perimeter of the property.

The car stopped in the VIP parking spot provided for her each time she visited. Millicent immediately exited and began her long stroll past the playing fields lined with international flags and toward the lone glass building standing like a satellite space station in vacuous outer space.

Mr. Smythe met Millicent as she entered the building.

"Ah, Millicent, so good of you to come on such short notice. I hope your flight was satisfactory?"

"Huh? Oh, yes. Uneventful, as usual, thank God," she answered with a self-conscious little laugh.

Today was far from Millicent's first visit to FIFA headquarters. Yet with each invitation she found her attention increasingly snagged by the sight of the glittering trophies showcased in their respective boxes like crystal jewels set in glass cases. The Golden Boot, The Golden Ball, The Golden Glove, and the winning World Cup trophies—all sparkled in their individual brilliance with more dazzle than Millicent could ever have imagined.

Mr. Smythe led Millicent by the arm to one of the big glass-encased boardrooms, and as he did so, he couldn't help but smile.

"They're quite resplendent, are they not?" he asked proudly.

"Oh, dear. Yes. Sorry. I get so distracted. No matter how many times I've seen them in my imagination, I'm awestruck by their present glory. Now I understand more fully why they say football's 'the beautiful game.'"

They chuckled together as they made their way toward the boardroom doors.

"Ready dear?"

"Ready as I'll ever be," Millicent responded with as much confidence as she could muster, which wasn't all that much if one were to actually listen beneath her words.

As the doors swung open, Millicent and Mr. Smythe entered the boardroom as if they were the Queen and Prince Philip of England. They strutted their way up to the top of the table at the opposite end of the room.

As Millicent passed the sea of seated men, one by one they stood, smiled warmly, and applauded her arrival. However, as Millicent was about to smile and acknowledge their generous greeting, the rubber on the bottom of her right British walker stuck to the rug and sent her spiraling forward, arse over tea kettle.

Later in the day when looking back at that moment, Millicent realized the best thing she could've done was immediately drop to the floor and acquiesce to the helpful hand of one of the security officers. But unfortunately, she didn't.

Instead, she found herself contorting her arms and torso in an insane gymnastics routine created to keep her from losing her balance altogether. At the time it seemed to Millicent as if the balletics must've lasted thirty minutes or more. Luckily after dancing passed three men, a fourth officer grabbed her by the waist and held her upright in his strong militarily-trained arms.

How mortifying!

"Is Mademoiselle all right?" he asked, while sweat began to appear on his bald head.

If they only knew. This is absolutely dreadful. How am I ever going to make it through this meeting?

Millicent finally found her land-legs and with her head lowered and her cheeks aflame, she took her seat to the left of Mr. Smythe.

"Mademoiselle Winthrop's fine. I, too, have recently tripped over the same bit of carpet. Please accept our apology, Millicent, for this embarrassment. We will certainly take care of that loose corner immediately," Mr. Smythe reassured.

Millicent, spectacles askew, peeked up from under her hat at the seated men only to see how concerned and caring they all appeared.

Mr. Smythe continued.

"We, of course, are all aware of Ms. Winthrop's skills as well as her past achievements for our organization. As chief of security I've asked her to meet with us today to discuss our more recent dilemma in Nürnberg, Germany."

Mr. Smythe turned his face toward her as if to invite her to say a few words, but all that came from her mouth was a shaky and meager "er, yes?"

Silence filled the room.

Oh, my God. They must all want me to say more. But what can I possibly tell them? That I don't remember a stitch about what I did on the last assignment? That I haven't a clue as to how to go about assisting them again? That I'm quite possibly an absolute fraud?

Mr. Smythe once again came to her rescue.

"Yes. Absolutely yes. Brilliant of you to say so, Millicent dear."

He faced the others.

"Ms. Winthrop's obviously a woman of few words and much action. I've no doubt."

Millicent slid down in her chair and listened intently to the narrative the security officers presented to her regarding Riccardo Stillitano, the victim in question. Suddenly her mind envisioned the entire crime as if it were projected as a documentary film on the screen of her imagination. Yet unlike those in the room, the pictures in Millicent's head weren't from the viewpoint of the young midfielder, but rather from that of the criminal himself.

She took the phone receiver off of the wall phone and let it dangle. Quickly she moved to stand in the dark behind the door. She felt herself seething with anger. Wait. I've something in my hand. What is it? Ah. Chloroform and a rag. I hear him approaching now. Soon he'll be mine for the asking.

For a moment Millicent forgot where she was. She'd wanted to yell out a warning to the victim, but it obviously wouldn't have done any good. This had all happened in the recent past.

"And you say no ransom note whatsoever was left at the time or has emerged since?" she asked.

"That's right," they all answered in unison.

Mr. Smythe searched her with a worried face. "Not only do we not have a note, we've no eye witnesses or important clues either."

"Gentlemen," Millicent began. "Of course I may be totally wrong here, I often am, but in my own humble opinion this is the job of the same criminal as with our last case in Madrid."

"But Madamoi—" interrupted one of the security personnel at the table.

"I know what you're going to say, sir," Millicent rushed forward. "And the fact that no ransom note was left at this time doesn't dismiss the fact that both these crimes resemble themselves to the letter. I'm going to need to investigate the locker room at Nürnberg's soccer stadium as soon as possible. Given how this beast operated last time, we've little time to waste."

"But Mademoiselle," yet another gentleman barged in, "we've already gone over the crime scene with a fine tooth comb. What makes you think you'll discover anything more than what we did?"

Millicent rose to her feet and grinned exuberantly as she made her way out of the boardroom doors.

"Holmes and Watson, dear gentlemen," she shouted excitedly as she reached for the doors. "Holmes and Watson!" Slam.

***

Venice, Italy

Alfredo Martolini went about his late afternoon activities, yet couldn't help but have Millicent's continued welfare on his mind. She'd been one of his first and most difficult cases since specializing in brain trauma and amnesiac disorders. His progress with other patients made him an expert in the field, but Millicent was thus far his Waterloo. He understood why her memory prior to her injury was compromised, but he was at a loss as to why she still had these memory blackouts, as she called them, so many years after the initial trauma.

As he prepared to go to the open market to purchase ingredients for his evening meal, he once again tried to piece all the information together. Millicent had happened to be in her California apartment when the earthquake hit. This he knew to be the truth. Yet in spite of all the research, no one so far had seemed to figure out exactly who Millicent was. For one thing, there'd been no record of a "Millicent Winthrop" before her arrival at the hospital.

And for another, Millicent knew her name, but not much else about herself or how she came to be in London after her injury. One thing was for certain, however. Millicent was most definitely English.

He was about to leave home when his telephone rang. On the fourth ring he picked it up.

"*Pronto.*"

"Dr. Martolini? Alfredo Martolini?" asked a mature woman's voice with an unquestionable American accent.

"Sì. Yes. This is Doctor Martolini. To whom am I speaking?"

"Oh, good. I hoped this was your number. I'm Aunt Kate, Millicent's friend," the tentative voice on the end of the line explained.

"Ah, yes. Aunt Kate. How are you? Is Millicent doing all right? We had quite a challenging session this morning." A spark of tension crept into the conversation.

"Well, I think so. Actually, I'm not sure. That's why I called you. Is Millicent there?"

"No, I'm afraid she isn't. She left here several hours ago to take a flight to Zurich. Did she not mention it to you?" Alfredo could feel his heart hammer in this chest.

"No, she didn't. And as you know, I'm concerned. I feel as if I'm somehow responsible for her, even though I know she's a grown woman with an above average intelligence and capable of managing on her own. But, she does find herself from time to time in the most peculiar situations, and I was calling to see if this might possibly be one of those times."

At this point Alfredo heard a hint of panic beneath Aunt Kate's words of concern. "Yes, Millicent is a worry," agreed Alfredo.

And I feel as responsible as you for her safety.

"Truly, Doctor, how's she doing? Is her memory improving at all?"

Alfredo wasn't sure exactly how to answer, even though he knew he had all the legal permission necessary to be as truthful with Aunt Kate as need be. He was clear he didn't want to reveal how often Millicent preoccupied his thinking, yet he felt compelled as Millicent's psychiatrist to keep Aunt Kate up to date on her friend's therapeutic journey.

"Millicent's progressing." He certainly didn't want to mention her increasing inability to remember even post accident events. "She no longer appears to be frightened by our therapy sessions, nor does she miss appointments or arrive late.

That's safe enough.

"And her self-confidence, though shaky at times, seems to be growing stronger with each visit. I believe it helps to have her bring Holmes and Watson along with her. They adore her, and she seems highly responsive to their every need."

Alfredo waited to hear Aunt Kate's voice on the other end of the line but only silence ensued.

"Hello? Aunt Kate, are you still there?" he asked.

He heard her clear her throat. "What I actually want to know, Doctor, is will she ever get well? I mean, in the head?"

That was the question, wasn't it? And in spite of all of his expertise, even Dr. Alfredo Martolini didn't have the foggiest as to how long it would take for Millicent's memory to come back, if at all.

Aunt Kate continued. "I worry about her taking on this position at FIFA. And I know Millicent worries, too. She seldom sleeps at night, and when she does, I can hear her talking non-stop as if to someone other than myself.

"Plus, she often leaves home or the hotel for interminable lengths of time without telling me where she has gone or when she's coming back. And excuse me for saying this, but I don't think her memory's improving one bit. In fact, I think she's losing whatever's left in that head of hers one wit at a time."

"I know, I know. I struggle with her working for FIFA as well. She seems so happy to have her mind occupied by something larger than herself, and yet I, too, am afraid for her safety," admitted Alfredo.

"So, what're you going to do about it?" Aunt Kate was losing her patience.

"Good question. I do keep in touch with Mr. Smythe daily, and he assures me Millicent's in good hands. Yet I'm not always so sure." Alfredo worried that he'd revealed far too much to Aunt Kate, but he wanted to be as honest and truthful as he could under the circumstances.

"Well, I'm not the only one responsible for Millicent. You and Mr. Smythe took this project on, putting Millicent in a most precarious of positions. She wants to please both of you so much that I often wonder how strongly she actually feels about solving these horrible crimes. It's time you recognized Millicent's more to you than a mere patient, for it's clear to me you're much more to her than a mere therapist."

With that the line went dead, leaving Alfredo holding the dial-tone-emitting receiver in his hand. It was true. Millicent had indeed become more to him than a mere patient, but what exactly that was, he had no idea.

Yet he understood Aunt Kate's concerns. He had them too. Millicent's safety and memory were in his hands. And it was time he admittedly did something about it.

Chapter 4

When Millicent finally arrived back at her suite in Venice, she immediately checked in on Holmes and Watson. It was barely past dusk, and yet it was obvious to her that Aunt Kate had done very little to either pick up after the boys or to take them out for their constitutional.

In fact, Millicent was rather surprised to discover Aunt Kate was nowhere to be found. But it was after all dinner time and knowing Aunt Kate the way she did, Millicent figured she'd most likely barricaded herself in her hotel room most of the day in order to avoid the afternoon heat and bustling crowds only to later possibly take an early evening stroll to a nearby trattoria or sidewalk café.

Millicent appropriately put Holmes and Watson on their leads and led them out for a brisk walk along the *Calle dell'Aseo*, passed the Coins department store, and toward the Teatro Goldoni. The boys loved this familiar trek and were most grateful to be out of their hotel room and into the fresh cool evening air.

"Don't keep us in suspense any longer, Millicent dear," said Holmes. "We've been waiting all afternoon for your return, and not very happily I might add."

"Yeah," added Watson, "not very 'appily indeed."

"Oh, my gracious," said Millicent. "I'm so sorry Aunt Kate wasn't more responsive to your needs, but I'm here now. Besides, this is your favorite area of Venice, and when we get back to the hotel, I will make sure you've a nice bowl of dog food to carry you over until tomorrow."

Holmes and Watson gazed at each other rather confused. Then Watson broke the silence by saying, "Yeah, dog food. *Woof.*"

Holmes glanced back at his mistress. He was obviously concerned but didn't want to show it. Millicent had enough on her mind these days without her worrying about him and Watson.

These two pugs had learned a longtime ago how to fend for themselves, as Millicent would often go for days on end before returning. But at least she always did. And luckily she'd lately taken the two of them with her to Venice rather than leave them at home in Nether Wallop, England.

And a very fine home it was, thought Holmes, as the three of them trotted along the *Campo San Luca*. The book-laden bungalow consisted of one bedroom, a bathroom with a tub, a lovely sitting area with a dining table, and a little tiny kitchen, barely big enough for a sink, an oven, a two burner cooker, and a European refrigerator. The flowered sofa was soft and comfy, as was the padded rocking chair in the corner where Millicent loved to sit and knit.

Sharing the dining area was Millicent's spinet piano, which she loved to play each evening before bed. On it were adorned a few pictures of Doctor Martolini, as well as Holmes and Watson, and various figurines and knick-knacks.

The tiny garden behind the cottage was filled with blooming plants and shrubs, and the thatch roof above the home's stone walls was likewise fragrant year round. Today, however, the three weren't in cozy England, but rather prancing along one of the many laundry-festooned streets of Venice.

"Please, Millicent, I'm afraid I can't wait much longer. Tell us all about your trip to FIFA headquarters," Holmes requested.

Both Millicent and Holmes waited a few seconds to allow Watson to say his usual, "Yeah, FIFA 'eadquarters," but it didn't come. The two of them searched back to where they had last seen Watson, and there he sat on a small stone bench next to a little boy who was at this moment sharing his *gelato al limon* with him—a spoon in one hand and a small cup of ice cream in the other. Watson's face was in a full pucker at the tartness of his sudden treat, and as perturbed as Holmes and Millicent were, they couldn't help but laugh.

"What?" said Watson or something which sounded somewhat like it.

Millicent giggled so hard, she thought she was going to wet herself. Holmes actually found a corner of a nearby building to do his piddle, but he, too, laughed despite his disgruntlement with his brother. Thinking he was in trouble, Watson immediately leapt toward the young boy, grabbed the gelato from the boy's hands with his mouth, and took off at a full gallop.

"Oh, drat," commented Holmes, whose attitude instantly sobered.

"Oh bother," Millicent echoed directly. "Watson, you come back here right now, you naughty boy." And with that, Millicent, Holmes, and the young boy took off after Watson as quickly as their legs could carry them.

Soon Holmes was in the lead. "Miss, it looks as if he is headed toward St Mark's Basilica. I will run ahead and attempt to cut him off. You and the young lad stay in pursuit. Don't worry, we'll catch up to him sooner or later." And off he went. Millicent quickened her step and caught up to the young boy who was beginning to cry.

"Don't worry about your gelato, young man. I'll get you another, but first you must help me catch that little scoundrel Watson."

The boy's eyes brightened. Even though Millicent's Italian wasn't all that good, the boy apparently understood enough English to know that all was not lost. With an ear-to-ear grin the boy took Millicent's hand.

"*Vieni con me!* Come with me, signorina! I think I know where he may go next."

Millicent knew she was in no place to argue, so off the two of them flew toward St. Mark's Square. They wound through many convoluted streets and neighborhoods until they arrived at a piazza filled with the aroma of many shops and cafes. Millicent and the boy stood in the middle and panned the area. Suddenly they heard what they were sure was the muffled bark of a short impish pug.

Millicent at first couldn't believe her eyes. There before her, running out of a delicatessen faster than he'd ever in his life was Watson with a trailing bouquet of tightly encased sausages hanging from his gelato-encrusted mouth. And hot at his heels chasing after him was an irate man in a white apron, obviously the owner of the neighborhood *gastronomia*, and two rather corpulent policemen who had coincidently been in the shop purchasing prosciutto slices for their evening dinner.

"*Fermate il ladro!* Stop! Thief!" the owner cried.

"*Fermare in nome della legge!* Stop in the name of the law!" the polizia echoed.

"Watson, put those sausages down and come here at once," Millicent and the boy yelled simultaneously.

Millicent knew Watson most likely didn't hear her above all the jeers, laughter, and whistle-blowing of the crowd. But she had to try. It was also clear to her by now that Watson wasn't having as much fun as he thought he would and was most assuredly in full panic mode.

Millicent and the boy dashed through the crowd trying hard to catch up with the errant pug. Then suddenly as if from nowhere, Holmes jumped out in front of Watson blocking his path. Watson tried to skid to a stop, but instead tumbled push face over curly tail across Holmes's sturdy back and landed on his tummy—all four of his legs sprawled out in every direction, which immediately threw him into three full three-hundred-and-sixty degree belly spins.

As soon as Watson came to a complete stop, Holmes retrieved the sausages from Watson's mouth and brought them over to the panting shop owner. Satisfied with the return of his goods, the man called off the police. Together everyone went back to the shop laughing and congratulating the owner and two policemen for a job well done.

Millicent, Holmes, and the boy raced over to where Watson lay.

"I'm sorry, Millicent," Watson whimpered, staring up into her face with his googly, sorrow-filled eyes. "When it comes to gelato and sausages, I'm 'fraid I can't 'elp meself."

A thousand things Millicent could've said in this moment, but because she knew Watson was already ashamed and sorry for what he'd done, she instead took him up into her arms. The four of them then made their way back to the boy's neighborhood.

"What's your name, young man?" Millicent asked in broken Italian.

No answer. Millicent continued.

"You know, it was very nice of you to offer your gelato to Watson. He seldom gets as nice a treat as you offered. And I'm sorry he took it from you. He was a bad boy." Watson wiggled and moaned ever so slightly in her arms. Holmes snorted.

"Tell you what, show me where you bought it, and I'll get each of us one as a special way of thanking you for your thoughtfulness."

"Paolo. My name's Paolo Ricci. And is it all right if my mamma comes with us too?"

"All right, Paolo. That sounds fair."

Within minutes Millicent, Holmes, and Watson stood in front of the massive wooden door of a stucco building just a few odd turns away from the main walkway. Paolo ran inside and soon he and his mother with purse in hand trotted with the others to the local gelato wagon.

Millicent didn't mind. In fact, she enjoyed Signora Ricci's company. The signora talked a mile a minute in rapid fire Italian, most of which Millicent didn't understand, nor did she try. She merely nodded and smiled generously as the five of them paraded through the busy neighborhood to the promised destination.

After the ice cream Paolo and his mamma bid Millicent and the two pugs *buona sera, ciao* to make their way back toward their home. Millicent,

Holmes and Watson did the same—retraced their steps back to the hotel with happy thoughts and contented tummies.

"Now Millicent, are you going to tell us about your trip or am I going to have to howl all night until you do?" Holmes asked sternly.

"Yeah, all night," echoed Watson.

Millicent couldn't help but grin.

"Of course, I will tell you everything before you go to bed, but first we must get back to our hotel before it gets dark. I'm a bit worried about Aunt Kate, so we must quicken our steps and make our way post haste."

Millicent picked up her pace. "What I will tell you is this. We're on a great assignment. Another footballer has been kidnapped, and this time his life may be in real danger."

Holmes and Watson gazed at each other with excited anticipation. This was what they'd both hoped for—a challenge to their wits of detection and the subsequent triumph of their mistress at her best.

"Woof!" remarked Holmes in response to Millicent's request.

"Yeah, woof!" rejoined Watson as he too accepted his new assignment.

***

The earlier phone call from Aunt Kate had disturbed Alfredo Martolini more than he'd wanted to admit. For one thing, something about the woman's voice sounded oddly familiar, as if he'd known her long before their initial introduction a year ago. And second, Aunt Kate was right—he had to do something, but exactly what that was he didn't know.

After hanging up the phone, he sat in his Italian leather arm chair, closed his eyes with his hands clasped, index fingers pressed against his forehead, and tried to think about his next move. If he called Millicent at her hotel, she may think he was checking up on her, and that would do absolutely nothing toward building up her self-esteem.

He could stop by her hotel on the pretense he was merely in the area and wanted to say hello, but he knew Millicent was too bright for that sort of nonsense. So again he let the notion slip back into wherever it came from.

Finally, he decided to leave a message at the concierge desk of the hotel asking Millicent to move their therapy session up a day so he could see her tomorrow instead of the morning after.

Perfetto! Millicent won't suspect anything out of the ordinary.

Feeling rather smug, Alfredo gathered his coat and headed toward the Rialto Bridge market where he could pick up a piece of fish, some tomatoes, an eggplant, and a loaf of crisp Italian bread to go with a bottle of delicious Valpolicella wine. He hadn't taken but two steps away from his door when he realized he had no idea what he'd say to Millicent when she arrived the next day. Yet he knew it would have to be said strong enough so she understood how much she meant to him, if not as a woman, *poi certo come il suo cliente*—then surely as his client.

Make Mine The Italian

***

Zurich, Switzerland

At dinner that evening Mr. Smythe's wife noticed her husband wasn't his usual attentive self.

"What's the matter with you tonight, Bucky? It's been a long time since I've seen you so locked within yourself."

"It's nothing new, my dear. The hostilities of this new criminal have escalated, and we at FIFA need Millicent's help now more than ever. Yet I'm worried about her. She seems so out of touch with reality, and yet so in touch with the way the criminal mind operates. I can only guarantee her safety up to a certain point, and then like her I'm vulnerable to whatever evil this monster may well generate."

Immediately he smashed his fist onto the table in front of him, and just as quickly Sabrina placed both her hands gently on his.

"Darling, I know how much you care for Millicent. We both do. She has a special place in our hearts. But she depends on you, Bucky, for like me she knows she can. You're the best detective in Europe if not the world, and it's only right you pass down your instincts, skills, and intelligence to someone young and smart, even if that someone's our dear sweet Millicent."

Mr. Smythe searched Sabrina's loving face.

She placed the palm of her hand on his cheek. "Between the two of you, I know this horrendous villain will be apprehended and brought to justice. And somewhere in your heart you know it too."

"You're right, dear wife. I only hope we do so before anyone gets hurt."

Or killed, he thought to himself.

"I love you Bucky."

"And I love you too, Sabrina."

He then got up from his chair, wrapped his arms around his wife, and pressed his lips against hers with all the assurance he could muster in that fragile moment.

Chapter 5

Venice, Italy

As soon as Millicent and the two pugs returned to the hotel suite, she noticed Aunt Kate's bedroom door was closed. This wasn't unusual behavior for Aunt Kate. She often went to bed early, slept in late, and took long afternoon naps. Millicent did not. Millicent's gears turned in her head all day and usually kept her awake each night.

Yet with all the travel and excitement of the day, Millicent was beginning to feel adrift.

"Excuse me, Millicent, but you still have not told Watson and me about your visit to FIFA? How is our dear friend, Mr. Smythe?"

Millicent knew better than to leave anything unsaid to Holmes. He was not only bright, but loyal, caring, and hyper-vigilant—as any good alpha-male should be.

"Bucky's fine and sends you both his regards."

"Jolly good," Holmes wedged in between mouthfuls of his supper.

"Yeah, jolly good," Watson echoed, still hungry in spite of the two dishes of *gelato al limon* and half of a sausage he'd consumed earlier.

Millicent continued. "It seems Mr. Smythe has given us a second chance, boys. Another footballer has gone missing, and FIFA has hired the three of us to find him and bring his abductor to justice."

"Jolly good as well," Holmes said, his mouth full.

"Yeah, as well," Watson mumbled with his nose buried deep in his food dish.

"I suppose I should be excited, too. Yet I must admit I'm not exactly sure where to begin. Mr. Smythe and I believe the villain to be the same as in our last case, but with a much stronger purpose behind his madness. As a result, Bucky's afraid for the life of our missing young man, as I am too."

Holmes raised his head up from his empty dog bowl. "You mustn't worry so, Millicent. Watson and I will track him down faster than you can shake a stick, which I wouldn't recommend as it usually causes Watson to lose whatever train of thought he has going for him.

"We managed to find the last footballer, didn't we? And he is now safe at home with his family and in the protective care of FIFA's Security Council. Therefore, we will also manage to find this young man and the evil creature who took him."

Holmes was always so confident, Millicent thought to herself. Why, if she had only one tenth of Holmes's positive attitude, nothing could hold her back from possessing one of the greatest detective minds of the twenty-first century. The world would then be a much better and safer place. No doubt about it.

"I suppose you're right, Holmes. As always," she said. "We'll get right on this case in the morning after a short visit with Dr. Martolini. But for now we'd better get to sleep as we've a busy day ahead of us."

Holmes and Watson followed Millicent into her bedroom suite and lay down in their respective beds. Holmes circled his cushion three times before finally surrendering to the coziness of his bed, while Watson rooted his head into his pillow several times before it finally gave in to him.

"Good night, boys," Millicent tenderly whispered.

"Good night, Millicent dear."

"Yeah, Millicent dear."

As Millicent changed into her high-neck, long-sleeved flannel nightgown and put herself to bed, all the sounds of the hotel suite were at last quiet, except for the combined snoring of Holmes and Watson and possibly Aunt Kate as well.

***

For a change Millicent had no trouble getting to sleep. Yet as her sleep continued, she could feel herself becoming more and more restless. At first her dreams were of her and Dr. Martolini in a gondola floating beneath the many ornate bridges which connect the islands of Venice.

Alfredo was about to lean over and kiss her when the next thing she knew, she was sitting at a Parisian sidewalk café drinking tea and eating a croissant about the size of her shoe. All this occurred while at the same time a strange older gentleman with a thick French accent accosted her.

"Bonjour, Mademoiselle. Do you mind if I sit here with you and share your table?"

My gracious, he's rather forward, even if it is my own dream.

"Uhhhhhh . . . ." Millicent was too shocked to come up with an answer. Besides, she had enough croissant stuffed in her mouth to muffle even the most articulate retort.

"You're Millicent Winthrop, are you not?" he asked as he plopped his grey wrinkled trench-coat-clad body into the chair next to hers.

She looked both ways to see if a gendarme was in sight or anyone else for that matter, but the café appeared to be deserted accept for the two of them. She reluctantly nodded her head and continued chewing.

"Allow me to introduce myself. I'm Monsieur H—pronounced "ahsh"—and I'm here to be of your assistance, dear lady."

"Monsieur Ahsh?"

"Oui, Mademoiselle, Inspector H with the Paris Sûreté. Perhaps you've heard of me, yes?"

Of course, I've heard of you, but for the life of me I can't remember where.

"Uhhhhhhh . . ."

"Mademoiselle Winth—, may I call you Millicent?"

Millicent pinched herself to make sure she wasn't dreaming.

"Ouch!" she shrieked.

"*Excusez-moi,* Mademoiselle." Monsieur H gazed at Millicent strangely. "I didn't mean to frighten you. I only want to help, if you will allow."

"Uhhh . . . *oui. Je* uh, *je* allow. *Oui.* And please, call me Millicent."

Gracious, my French's even worse than my Italian. You would think when a person dreamed they could at least speak perfectly in whatever language it was they were attempting to speak.

"*Trés bien,*" he said. Millicent it is."

Now, normally Millicent would be scared out of her wits—sitting in the middle of some unfamiliar Parisian suburb, speaking with a total stranger. But something about the way his kind dark eyes twinkled and the quiet authority in his voice somehow reassured Millicent he was undoubtedly safe enough, even if he was a Frenchman.

Now, why would I think that? I don't even know any Frenchmen. I guess it must be because I'm English. At least, I think I'm English. Oh, heavens. I don't for the life of me remember anymore.

"Perhaps you're afraid of me because I'm a Frenchman, *n'est pas*?"

Wow! How'd he do that?

"Truthfully, I'm not sure what's going on. I'd barely turned off my bedroom nightlight, when I found myself in a gondola with my psychiatrist, and now I'm here with you in the middle of the afternoon in Paris."

Millicent was sure that what she was experiencing wasn't her usual memory slip. But what it was exactly, she didn't know.

"I can appreciate the feeling," he continued. "I'm after all only an imaginary character, therefore I appear only in the minds of those who've read the stories of my adventures or perhaps need my assistance in solving particularly challenging crimes."

Something niggled at Millicent's memory. She was sure she'd heard of this man, but where and how she was at a loss.

"Of course, I remember you now," she fibbed. "I suppose that's why we're meeting here at an outdoor Parisian café as opposed to my private bedroom suite at the Hotel al Ponte Antico."

"*Mon dieu*, Mademoiselle, I would never think to impose."

You know, Millicent, sometimes you act like an utter fool, she thought, chiding her self.

It was difficult to tell who was turning more red, Inspector H or Millicent.

Make Mine The Italian

Can a person actually turn red if it's only a dream?

Since her accident, Millicent had difficulty remembering certain facts, and apparently one was whether someone dreams in color or not was one of them. Besides, in spite her "private bedroom" insinuation, it seemed beyond strange that she should have to meet Monsieur H anywhere but in her suite. But, it was his dream as much as hers and remembering that, Millicent decided to refrain from stressing over such a minor point as to whose turf they were actually meeting on.

"No imposition at all, Inspector. I'm sorry if I embarrassed you. I often say the most ridiculously inappropriate things when I'm nervous. I meant you no disrespect."

Millicent searched his face to see if she'd been forgiven. *Nothing's worse*, she reminded herself, *than getting off to a bad start when a novice detective meets another much more experienced and illustrious.*

Millicent wasn't sure how she knew that—she just did.

"I understand you're working on the missing person case of one Riccardo Stillitano, *n'est pas?*" Inspector H didn't seem to be overly upset by her earlier faux pas, so she decided to go ahead and take advantage of his presence by discussing what she could about the case.

"Yes, I fly into Nürnberg tomorrow to inspect the scene of the crime. Holmes and Watson, my two therapy pugs, will travel with me. I realize the Nürnberg police as well as Mr. Smythe's people at FIFA have already gone over the stadium's clubhouse with a fine toothed comb, but it has been my experience, though limited, that the experts often miss the most obvious of details. Details which are easy for my dogs to pick up. Unlike most humans, Holmes and Watson have very keen noses, what there are of them."

"Ah, ha. A very shrewd move indeed," affirmed the inspector, as he pulled out from his pocket a mysterious looking packet. He shook out a few of the blackest looking cigarettes her fixated eyes had ever seen. She'd heard about French cigarettes, especially those favored by Parisians, but she'd never had the opportunity to try one.

Seeing Millicent eye his Galois, Inspector H did as any true gentleman would. "Perhaps you care for a cigarette, Millicent dear?"

Millicent had never smoked anything in her life, at least, not as far as she could remember. Yet she was after all in Paris, *and when in Rome* . . . . *Oh what the hell, Viva la France!*

"*Absolutement. Merci*, Monsieur."

The inspector then struck a wooden match against the bottom of his worn down left shoe and lit Millicent's cigarette first before lighting his own. After passing it over, he took in a deep drag of his own and slowly blew smoke rings into the air above.

Millicent then proceeded to do the same. She took in a deep breath, but instead of provocatively dispensing with the pungent smoke from her lungs in wafting clouds of smoke, she began to sputter and choke. She strangled so hard she felt as if she was being strangled. Her eyes watered and her body shook as she gasped for air.

All this time, of course, Millicent pretended nothing unusual was happening to her. After all, this is what always occurred whenever she puffed on a cigarette.

She continued to smile brilliantly, all the while coughing as inconspicuously as she could into her serviette. Inspector H rushed out of his seat to stand behind her. He fastidiously lifted her arms above her head and pounded firmly but not too much so between her shoulder blades. The flower on Millicent's hat flopped vigorously forward and back on the top of her head. When Millicent finally calmed down, he then handed her his pocket handkerchief as well as the lukewarm cup of tea in front of her, which she drank down as quickly as she could.

"Yes," Millicent finally croaked, "a very shrewd move indeed."

Inspector H liked Millicent's quirkiness. Like so many others, he likewise found her refreshing. But he hadn't appeared tonight in her sleep merely to chat.

"Millicent, if you wouldn't mind, let's get back to the case."

Millicent put out her cigarette in the empty teacup, blew her nose on what was left of Inspector H's handkerchief, and nodded affirmatively.

"Do you have anyone you suspect?" he asked curiously.

"Not really, no," she said as she handed it back to him.

"Yet many similarities do exist between this case and the one I recently completed. Both victims were European football professionals, and even though the first case involved a ransom note, my suspicion is that because we rescued the young man minutes before he was nearly killed, the villain this time around isn't going to give us any opportunity for a clue such as was the earlier ransom note."

Millicent wanted to say more, but she wasn't sure how the inspector would take to the fact she was able to see these crimes from the criminal's point of view. And because of that talent more than anything else, Millicent was convinced the same man who kidnapped the first footballer was most assuredly the same one who was involved in this current case.

"I see. And have you any idea of the criminal's motivation?"

Millicent knew it was only a matter of time before she would spill the beans as to her unusual talent.

"I *sense* whoever did these crimes was an enraged and dark-souled individual, who at some time in his life must've been so utterly traumatized he now sees no other way to expunge his grief but to lash out violently."

Inspector H stared at Millicent with his dark penetrating eyes. "And you *sense* this how?"

"Uh . . ."

"Never mind, Mademoiselle." He threw his free hand into the air as if to karate chop the tension while simultaneously slicing through the thickened cigarette smoke. "Let us together at this time go over each of the clues as we know them."

Phew. I don't want this man to think I'm nuts so early in our introduction, even if he is a hallucination.

The inspector continued. "Both of these victims are professional football stars, *n'est pas?*"

"*Oui,*" Millicent answered swiftly.

"And both were kidnapped at their respective home team stadiums during a heavily attended afternoon's game."

"*Oui,*" Millicent answered firmly, feeling as if she were back in preparatory school answering test questions out loud in class in order to show off her brilliance for not only the teacher, but for her peers as well.

"And both were duped by answering what they thought were emergency phone calls from home," Millicent said as she took up the pace.

"Ah," Inspector H retorted with a smile.

"But as far as Mr. Smythe has determined, neither of the two young men knew each other personally. They'd never met, nor had they ever once played a game against one another."

"Interesting," continued the inspector. "So, perhaps the villain may be someone whom both these gentlemen have met in the past, *n'est pas?*"

"Perhaps."

Millicent didn't know why she felt the way she did, but she sensed the kidnapper's motivation had been far darker than any personal attack or misunderstanding between him and his victims. Suddenly she felt quite agitated, which in turn stimulated a series of more than a dozen nearly imperceptive sneezes.

Ah-choo!

Ah-choo!

Ah-Choo!

"*A tes souhaits,* Mademoiselle. Are you feeling ill?" the Inspector asked.

"*Ah-choo. Ah-choo. Ah-choo.*" Millicent continued.

"You must be upset about something. Please tell me what it is. In the meantime, I will lick your face. For I cannot resist."

Eww.

Why would this man even for a moment consider licking my face . . .

Ah-choo.

Millicent woke up at once to a room filled with sunlight and two insistent pugs licking what strangely looked like croissant crumbs from off her chin.

Chapter 6

An Undisclosed Location Somewhere in Europe

With his wrists shackled to the cold wall, midfielder Riccardo Stillitano could feel that his feet and lower legs were submerged in water. He tried to move his arms and twist his body, but to no avail. The air smelled dank and musty. Through the open window high above and to the right shone a ray of moonlight—almost enough for him to make out his dismal surroundings.

Over in the corner a swarm of rats inched their way around the edge of the muddied floor. If he wasn't mistaken, this place appeared much like a dungeon—an abandoned basement within an old building. Even the chained handcuffs dated back to the eighteenth century or earlier.

He tried to think, but his head was still pounding from whatever it was that knocked him out. And his empty stomach told him he must've been in and out of consciousness for at least two, maybe three days. He repeatedly called out for help, but the quietness of the building told him he was alone.

Who's done this to me? And why? What could I have possibly done to deserve this?

Riccardo wracked his brain trying to come up with the answers. All he could do was repeat again and again in his mind the events leading up to his abduction and entrapment. He vaguely remembered riding for what seemed an eternity in the back of some kind of van or big truck, but he couldn't tell for sure which make or model. He also believed he'd been transported part way by boat, but he wasn't certain for he'd completely passed out while en route.

Riccardo also remembered hearing a man's voice speaking in a language he'd heard before but was unfamiliar with. He'd not seen the man, however, as he was blindfolded. Nor did he have the slightest idea where the man had taken him. His only landmark was the insistent hourly tolling of nearby church bells outside his prison window. If he was right, it was now close to two AM.

I know this place, but for the life of me, it isn't coming. Oh, mio Dio, my head!

When he was about to pass out again, he heard someone stop outside

63

the window. Riccardo listened quietly. After a moment of silence, he heard footsteps on the stairs making their way toward him. His heart began to race. Keys jingled in the locked door of his cell and the wooden door opened with a creak. There standing in the threshold was the outline of a huge, muscularly built man with slicked-back hair. As the stranger slid into the moonlit room, Riccardo could make out his light brown hair, long nose, and piercing blue eyes.

"Ah, Signor Stillitano, I see you're finally awake. Permit me to introduce myself more formally. My name's Vasilov Bugár, and I am the last person you'll ever see before your untimely death."

***

Venice, Italy

Millicent knew if she wanted to be in Nürnberg early by this afternoon, she needed to get herself and the pugs over to Dr. Martolini's as soon as possible. He had told her when she rang earlier that morning to be at his office by ten and no sooner, as he had a nine o'clock session with a new client, and he didn't want the two of them disturbed by one of her usual charming yet distracting entrances.

Once again Millicent bid Aunt Kate adieu, put the dogs on leash, and headed in the direction of the Dorsoduro. "My dear, Millicent," began Holmes as he trotted down the *Calle dell Ovo*, "how is it you were found to have numerous crumbs from a Parisian croissant affixed to your chin as you awoke this morning, when we all know you were miles away in Zurich yesterday and did not leave our room last night once you'd arrived?"

"Yeah, once you'd arrived," Watson chimed in.

Careful not to let the dogs on to her own concerns, Millicent answered Holmes as nonchalantly as she could.

"That's exactly the question I wish to pose to Doctor Martolini this morning. I can't believe I would've sleepwalked myself all the way to Paris, or a Parisian bakery here in Venice for that matter, for a mere croissant. And if I did, surely one would think I'd remember such a thing."

Holmes and Watson turned their heads toward each other and rolled their eyes. They knew all too well how forgetful Millicent could be, yet even this behavior seemed odder than usual.

"Perhaps you got up in the middle of the night and noshed on one of Aunt Kate's goodies. She hides them all over the suite, you know." Holmes said, doing his best to quell Millicent's anxiety.

"Yeah, all over the suite," Watson interjected. "She says she's on a diet, which is why she 'ides them from even 'erself. But I know where they're 'idden, and so does 'olmes. Maybe you do, too?" Watson rarely said more than three or four words at a time, but when he did, his words took on a meaning all their own.

Millicent still seemed perplexed. "Perhaps, but why a croissant? And why in the middle of the night of all things? After all, I'm on a new dietary regime, you know."

Holmes rolled his eyes for a second time. No matter how many sweets Millicent ate, she always claimed to be on a diet. "Maybe it was a dream?"

"Yeah, a dr—" Watson, as usual, was interrupted.

"Yes, that's it." The images of last night's dream flooded Millicent's consciousness. "I remember now. I dreamt I sat at an open air café in the center of Paris, sipping tea, and eating the most delicious croissant. And I wasn't alone. Yes, there was also a man in my dream—a Monsieur Ah-Choo, no that's not right, a Monsieur Ah-Shoe. No, that's still not correct." Millicent went silent for a few seconds.

"Ahsh. That's it. His name was Inspector H, and he wanted to discuss with me the Nürnberg case. Huh. How strange."

"Strange indeed. But a dream still doesn't explain how it is you found yourself this morning camouflaged in croissant crumbs," Holmes remarked. He was always such a stickler for detail.

"Yeah, croissant crumbs," Watson added.

Millicent and the pugs were about to cross the Accademia Bridge when Watson all of a sudden began barking ferociously.

"What is it Watson? What's going on?"

Millicent could barely hang on to Watson's lead. Then Holmes likewise started to carry on in the same manner.

"What is it, Holmes? Is someone in trouble?" she asked in a panic.

Both Holmes and Watson together pulled hard on their leads, dragging Millicent away from her familiar route to Dr. Martolini's and instead toward a shabby-looking chapel a few blocks southeast of where the commotion had begun. For blocks Millicent worked hard to control the two pugs. Instead they broke loose of her hold and ran toward an old church building barking as ferociously as they could with Millicent in full chase.

"Stop, Holmes. Come here this minute, Watson. Please, tell me what's going on?" she shrieked, chasing after them.

But the two pugs took off as if on a fox hunt. Millicent knew this behavior wasn't unusual if they'd indeed tracked a rat or a kitten or even freshly made sausages, for that matter. Yet this current free-for-all was somehow out of order, if not by its very intensity.

Terrace windows from the nearby buildings opened and people began to call out: *"Qual è il problema?"* What's the matter? *"Perché c'è così tanto abbaiare?"* Why's there so much barking? *"Non può tenere quei cani tranquillo?"* Can't you keep those dogs quiet? *"Non lo sai che questa è la casa di Dio?"* Don't you know this is a house of God?

"Ci dispiace. Sorry," Millicent said, unable to think of what else to say. Embarrassed out of her mind, she finally gathered Holmes and Watson together, but not before Watson in full view decided to lift his leg and tinkle on the front façade of the beautifully ornate chapel.

She was all set to scold the two pugs, when the church bells suddenly began to toll the ten o'clock hour. Now on top of everything else they were late for their appointment with Dr. Martolini.

This day is definitely not starting out well. Not at all.

"So sorry, Millicent, dear. We couldn't help ourselves." Holmes felt truly repentant, Watson not so much.

"Yeah, 'elp ourselves."

"We will discuss this matter after our appointment with Dr. Martolini. Thanks to you, we are now late, and you know how upset I can get when I'm late," she sputtered.

Holmes and Watson trotted the rest of the way with their heads hanging down. They knew they were in trouble, but they also knew something wasn't right in that church building. Holmes decided to convince Millicent and Watson to return for a better look as soon as they could.

***

The morning had been more difficult than usual for Alfredo. He'd planned to spend a pleasant morning with his mother Emilia, taking her first to mass and then to market, but a late night call from a suicidal new client had turned his plans upside down. He had wanted to tell the man he was unavailable, but Alfredo's curiosity got the best of him when he'd heard the anger and desperation in the man's voice.

Then on top of everything else was the six AM phone call from Millicent begging him for one more short session before taking off for Nürnberg where her services were needed at the scene of the latest crime. No matter what his plans, however, Alfredo knew in his heart he would always go out of his way to find time for his favorite client and her two canine friends. Why that was, he couldn't say, but the woman definitely had his attention in more ways than even he could define.

He'd barely finished putting on his jacket and combing his hair into place when he heard a loud rap at his office door. He checked the clock. It was only eight-thirty, far too early for either Millicent or his new client.

"Signor Martolini, open the door. I need to see you now." The booming voice of a heavily accented man bellowed from the top of Alfredo's staircase outside his office door.

"Who are you and what do you want?" Dr. Martolini was a man accustomed to being treated with utmost respect, not some servant waiting at the beck and call of an aggressive master.

"I'm your appointment. I came early for I didn't think an hour would be enough time for you to take care of my problem," the voice shouted back with great force.

For the love of Mary, who does this guy think he is?

"Okay. Okay. *Basta un minuto perfavore.* Please, one minute." Alfredo could tell already this was going to be an exceptionally long day.

69

The battering of the door continued loudly as the doctor moved patiently toward the locked door. As soon as his key turned in the dead bolt, a disheveled man barged past Alfredo, nearly knocking him to the floor. Dr. Martolini quickly sized up the situation. After all, it wasn't exactly clear how much danger if any he may be in.

The man was clearly distraught. He was in a severely wrinkled white suit, as if it had somehow gotten wet and then been slept in. His face was unshaven, and Alfredo wasn't positive, but he could swear the man's hands were bruised and his knuckles scraped.

"I apologize *Doktor* Martolini for my rude behavior. I'm not myself lately. I can't eat. I can't sleep. And I can't think clearly for more than a few minutes at a time. I don't know how much longer I'll be able to continue swimming in this whirlpool of desperation. I beg you, sir, please help me."

Alfredo wasn't sure if he should invite the man in or call *la polizia*. Finally, he offered his hand.

"Please come in. Would you prefer to sit or lay on the couch?" Obviously, Alfredo could see the man was agitated, but perhaps by lighting on a piece of furniture for a few moments, the man would calm him down long enough for the two of them to have a conversation.

Wrong. The stranger strode around the room at a fierce pace, first looking out the south window, then the one facing east. Finally, he opened the door and peered down the upstairs hallway as if he were sure someone unwanted was listening in on him.

"Sorry, *doktor*. I'm far too upset to remain in one place. Perhaps I shouldn't have come after all," the man said, clearly stressed.

Alfredo felt truly concerned for the man's manic behavior. "No. No, please signore. Don't go yet. We haven't even had a chance to get to know each other." Alfredo continued to offer his hand.

"I'm Doctor Alfredo Martolini. And you are?"

The man momentarily stopped in his tracks, ignoring the doctor's proffered hand.

"It doesn't matter what my name is. I've a very large problem, and I was told you could help me solve it," he nearly shouted.

Alfredo put his hand on the man's left shoulder. "I'll be glad to, if I can. Please, sit."

With those words the man finally demonstrated only minimal signs of calming down. He sat on the edge of the leather chaise and ran his hands through his stringy but matted hair. Alfredo thought he actually saw pieces of seaweed stuck to the man's scalp and hairline.

"*Doktor*, I'm sorry for this intrusion. But I'm not doing well, not well at all. Currently, I'm but a visitor to your fair city doing business, but I was born in Srebrenica.

"I came to Venice as a refugee nearly twenty years ago to live with an uncle who has since passed away, but I left shortly thereafter. I was only fourteen at the time, but I had seen and experienced more than most children my age."

Alfredo vaguely remembered details of the war in the former Yugoslavia during the early years of the 1990s. He was a young boy himself when the Bosnian war had taken place. It'd been an evil war, filled with ethnic cleansing on the part of the Serbs against their Muslim Bosniak friends and neighbors, as well as all manner of atrocities committed by both sides of the fighting.

"Where are you now living? With your family?" Alfredo asked, sitting in his favorite chair.

"I've no family. I lost everyone but my uncle in the war—my father, my mother and my older sister. I'm now a man without a country to call my own." He rose again from the comfortable harbor of the soft leather chaise and headed toward the window with its view of Venice proper.

The silence in the room was deafening as Alfredo waited for the man to continue. He wasn't immediately forthcoming, and the kind doctor didn't seem to want to push him given his unclear mental and emotional state.

Then with little or no emotion the man continued. "The year was 1995 during the early days of the month of July. My family had suffered much during the previous four years of that shit war, but we were still alive and together in what we felt was the safest place to be—the U.N. protected area of Srebrenica. And we weren't alone. At least 8,000 of our countrymen and women lived within the perimeter of what we hoped and prayed was the most secure of all places to be during that time."

He laughed sarcastically.

"One night our sleep was interrupted by the sound of soldiers coming into our encampment. My mother told my sister and me to run and hide as these armed men weren't a part of the United Nations militia. My father had once showed me a place in the back of the huge building where many Bosniak families like us were lodged."

The man paused to take in a short breath. "The back wall had a crack in the plaster, revealing a tiny space where a little child could crawl into and hide without being seen. He'd told me if for any reason I should feel unsafe, I was to go to this place and stay until either he or my mother said it was all right for me to come out."

The room grew quiet once again as the man voyaged back in time to his childhood. The only force keeping his fragile psyche from falling apart was the silence between the two men. Alfredo had at first believed he should convey words of sympathy or perhaps encouragement, but thought better of it as the silence continued. At last the man turned toward him and spoke.

"Don't you want to know what happened next, *doktor*? Are you not curious as to why I'm telling you this sad story?"

Make Mine The Italian

The man stared hungrily into the eyes of the doctor. His voice saturated with both sadness and anger. The ferocity in his face was so great his features hardened into the appearance of a death mask.

"*Sì prega di continuare* signore." As gently as he could, Alfredo encouraged his new patient to continue.

The man's words then spilled out of his mouth with such quiet severity that the atmosphere in the room had gone from pure rage to utter anguish.

"My sister refused to leave my mother's side. I know this because through a tiny gap in the wall I was able to see everything. First men came into the shelter and surrounded us with their soldiers and their guns. The command was for all the Bosniak men and boys to stand up and follow them out into the night air."

Alfredo detected a slight tremor in the man's voice. "My mother began to cry out, 'No, please, for the love of God who gave you life, don't take our husbands, brothers, and sons.' Instantly the officer in charge commanded one of his men to strike my mother's cheek with his rifle butt. As she fell to the ground, my father ran toward her. As he did, the same soldier shot him point blank through his forehead."

The man again laughed sardonically. "Funny isn't it *doktor*, how the human being can be shot dead and never bleed a drop, and yet someone struck in the head with a weapon will spill enough blood to flood an entire room? My sister immediately fell to her knees in tears, knowing that she most likely was their next victim."

Alfredo's face grew hot and tightened. Tears came to his eyes as he felt his breakfast begin to come up. He'd listened to many horrific stories in his adult life as a psychiatrist, but never one as devastatingly brutal as this. The man continued.

"I was too scared to move. I wanted to help my sister, but all I could do was piss my pants. Then the commander made his way over to my sister and forced her to her feet. He then shoved her toward his second in command and told him to take her to command headquarters.

"As she was escorted from the room, the remaining men and boys followed her lead. As soon as they shut and barricaded our door, the girls and women began to weep and wail. Some came to attend my mother who was half conscious by then, but I didn't move. Not one inch."

The man broke his gaze, turned away from Alfredo, and strolled back to the window where he'd first begun his recounting. He fished inside his pocket for a cigarette and lit it. Several minutes went by in silence as the man smoked. Finally, when the cigarette had burned down to half its length, the man opened the window and flicked what was left into the canal below.

"It has been over twenty years since that event took place and I'm still tormented by it. Not by my father's murder, or mother's assault or my sister's abduction, but by my own stupid inability to stop these men rather than wet myself."

Quickly he turned toward Alfredo, his eyes glazed over.

"I tell you this, *doktor*. I'm unable to eat or sleep or stop until I see justice done for what happened to my family. I will take my revenge any way I can or my soul will take its revenge on me. I care not who or what gets in my way—it's all the same to me. They all shall die!"

With that the man headed directly toward Alfredo's office door.

"Please wait, signore. Tell me before you go, what happened to your mother and your sister?"

"My sister was raped that evening by so many drunken soldiers she lost her mind. I found out later she'd been forgotten about and merely wandered away from the camp. She was never seen alive again. The men and boys had all been shot and buried in one mass grave. The next morning when the news came to us by way of the U.N., my mother did the only thing she could do—she hung herself."

The man then abruptly turned, marched through the threshold of the door, and slammed it behind him as he left.

Chapter 7

By the time Millicent along with Holmes and Watson arrived at Dr. Martolini's, she was worn out. Her hat was askew and her hair had already sprung loose from the tightly pinned chignon at the base of her neck.

Before Dr. Martolini noticed what a mess she'd become, Millicent quickly rearranged herself by tucking her blouse back into her skirt and by slipping her feet out of her shoes to try and rub off the scuff marks prominently displayed on her British walkers. She then readjusted her jacket, replaced her shoes, and then breathed heavily onto her spectacle lenses only to give them a final polish with the hem of her half slip before returning them to the bridge of her nose.

Normally it was all she could do to keep Holmes and Watson from hurtling her toward the handsome psychiatrist's office, but today she uncustomarily had to drag them by the leash. Something back at that chapel had caught their attention but good.

No sooner had the three opened the door to the Doctor's home, but a beefy man came careening down the stairs nearly mowing them over. Millicent lost her grip on the dog's leads while Holmes and Watson simultaneously barked wildly while jumping up onto the man's legs as best they could.

Dr. Martolini in the meantime in hot pursuit had run down the stairs as well . . . yelling, "Wait, signore. Please."

By the time Alfredo reached Millicent, however, the man had disappeared down one of the many canal promenades. Holmes and Watson, barking in excitement, ran back toward Dr. Martolini and madly encircled him and Millicent. Holmes clockwise, Watson counterclockwise. Soon their entangled leashes forced Millicent to once again lose her balance and fall, this time into the strong arms of her hero. Uh . . . doctor, that is.

Millicent gazed up into Alfredo's face. She'd never seen him so disheveled, which was completely out of character for the man was known for his fastidiousness.

"Oh, my," she exclaimed without thinking.

A slight hint of perspiration collected above his lower lip and his normally combed hair was sexily hanging loose from his forehead. His arms held her so tightly against his body, she knew if he let her go now, her rubbery legs would see her sliding down his well-developed muscular body and into a heap at his feet.

She began to hyperventilate.

Finally, Alfredo lowered his searching eyes down onto Millicent. He, too, was aware of this wisp of a woman firmly pressed to the front of his body. Alfredo knew if she were any one of another of his patients, he would've let her go by now, but for some odd reason he plainly didn't want to.

In fact, he was beginning to feel as if he wanted to kiss her, and not just on that cute little pouty mouth of hers either. As he began to bend his head toward Millicent with that very intention in mind, Millicent stiffened ever so slightly and said with a smirk, "Remind me to never again leave one of our sessions without paying you. You'd probably chase me all the way back to England."

The awkwardness of the moment was immediately assuaged by a loud burst of laughter from the doctor. Alfredo gently released Millicent, took out his handkerchief from his hip pants pocket, and wiped his lip and brow. Millicent quickly adjusted her hat, spectacles, and clothes, all the while finding her sea legs.

"Bad puppies," she said trying to make her voice sound firm, but no sooner had the words left her mouth, but she started to get the giggles. And basically couldn't stop. "I absolutely don't know what has gotten into these boys today. First the church and now this. Oh, my gracious. And I can't seem to stop laughing no matter how hard I try. Tee-hee-hee."

First of all, Millicent knew most of her laughter was due to her frayed nerves from being held so long in Doctor Alfredo Martolini's arms.

He wasn't actually going to kiss me. Or was he?

Second, it was clear something strange was going on at the chapel earlier, but she didn't have a clue as to what.

And third, what was it that possessed Holmes and Watson to behave in such an unruly manner?

***

Alfredo finally stopped laughing as he swept the hair off his forehead and back into place. He considered for a moment what had transpired, not only between him and his mysterious client, but more importantly, between him and Millicent.

I wasn't actually going to kiss her. Or was I?

Finally he cleared his throat to speak. "I'm sorry for the behavior of the gentleman leaving my office, signorina. I'm sure his behavior upset *I miei fratellini carlini*. For a brief moment they must've felt you were unsafe. And for that I also ask your forgiveness." His eyes turned from a professional dark brown to a luscious and ever so sexy Lamborghini black.

"Uh ... um ... okay. Sure." Her simple grin now appeared like a piece of freeze-dried fruit.

When he felt Millicent stiffen, Alfredo suddenly became aware of the impropriety of the situation and released Millicent from his gaze as well as his arms.

"Come, *carlini*. Time for amoretti. *Sì?*" he asked in an effort to change the atmosphere. Holmes and Watson ascended the marble staircase and prepared themselves for Millicent's morning session with the doctor. He then turned around once again toward Millicent, his eyes returning to their clinical dark brown.

***

"Signorina Winthrop?" Alfredo motioned for Millicent to obediently follow the boys up the stairs and into his familiar office.

"Oh, yes. Well, of course." Millicent couldn't remember how it was she was able to propel her unresponsive body forward, but somehow she made it up the staircase, down the narrow hallway, and into his office which now felt completely alien to her.

As she adjusted herself on his couch, Millicent's pulse throbbed beneath her reddened cheeks. Whatever was happening to her was a new, nerve-wracking, downright frightening, absolutely terrifying experience. Yet at the same time unspeakably delicious.

"Ahhhhhh!" Without thinking, Millicent let out a breathy sigh and stretched out onto the soft leather chaise.

Dr. Martolini already seated in his tapestried side chair peeked up from his notes.

"You're sleepy, signorina?"

Holmes and Watson gazed up from their water dish, moisture dripping off of their nonexistent chins. Holmes barked a short warning to remind Millicent as to where she was and what it was she was supposed to be doing. Watson followed with a wet sneeze.

"Oh, yes. I mean, no. I'm not sleepy, but I did have a very strange dream last night, which I want to relate to you before I leave this morning for Nürnberg."

"Please, signorina. Tell me what you remember."

Alfredo adjusted himself in his chair, his eyes half closed as Millicent recounted her meeting with Inspector H the night before in her dreams. Meanwhile, Holmes and Watson cozied themselves into their temporary dog bed, still panting, their tongues nearly touching the floor.

***

The silence was deafening as Millicent and the two pugs made their way back toward their hotel. Finally, Holmes cleared his throat.

"I say, Millicent dear, why is it you did not inform Dr. Martolini about waking this morning with a face full of crumbs? Is that not why you made the appointment in the first place?"

Holmes was always curious, especially with matters concerning Millicent's nutritional health.

"Yeah, crumbs." And whatever made Holmes curious, Watson followed suit.

The three of them had hastily left the doctor's appointment nearly half of an hour before the normally allotted time. Once Millicent finally settled down from her collision with the handsome Dr. Martolini, it didn't take long for her to once again become fidgety and restless.

"I don't wish to talk about it. I'd simply finished speaking to the doctor, and so we left. End of sentence."

Holmes and Watson turned their heads toward each other for a brief moment in silence. Finally, Watson spoke.

"Yeah, but what about the crumbs? Remember 'the crumbs?' What about the crumbs?"

Millicent felt her cheeks redden with embarrassment as they sauntered along the canal streets toward the Accademia Bridge.

What's it about those bloody crumbs? How could I've forgotten why it was I needed to see Dr. Martolini?

"Never mind about the crumbs, or the appointment, or Inspector H, for that matter. I merely ended our appointment when it became apparent, at least to me, that Dr. Martolini wasn't listening to a single word I was saying. He might as well have been missing from the room entirely. I pay far too much as it is to have the doctor check out on me."

Holmes cleared his throat.

"Millicent, dear, I believe Mr. Smythe and FIFA are making compensation for your therapy sessions, not you."

Millicent stopped abruptly in the middle of the crowded piazza in front of the bridge.

"That's beside the point. I don't care who's paying for what. What I *do* care about is having someone for whom I care deeply ignore me and my feelings. Bloody hell, just because he's good-looking doesn't mean he can step all over my heart—I mean my session time."

Holmes and Watson lowered their heads and not necessarily because they felt ashamed by their persistent questioning. People passing gave Millicent strange looks as she continued speaking and rather loudly to the non-existent voices only she seemed to hear. Holmes, more than Watson, understood that even though the pugs were able to interpret what people said to them, Millicent was the only human able to hear Holmes and Watson speak as well as comprehend what they were saying.

Most often this was a good thing, generally speaking. However, at this particular moment, things were growing a bit dicey. At last Holmes pulled on his and Watson's leash and off they went with Millicent paragliding behind them, hanging on for dear life.

"Come, Millicent. We'd better move ourselves along or we're going to miss our flight to Nürnberg."

"Yeah, Nürnberg."

And with that Millicent and the pugs soared across the bridge and back to their hotel to ready themselves for the rest of their day's adventure.

***

No sooner had Millicent left his office than Alfredo realized what he'd done. Drifted off into his own thoughts rather than listen to Millicent's most recent tribulation. This certainly wasn't his normal behavior, but then again, today wasn't his usual sort of day. First there was the strange man with the accent, who the more he thought about it appeared to be far more dangerous than first imagined.

The man's cold eyes showed little or no emotion, even when he spoke of his sister. And his affable smile seemed to appear and disappear far too easily for his charm to be taken with any shred of honesty. Even Holmes and Watson felt overly protective of Millicent as the man ran out of his office and disappeared between the buildings of the winding canal streets of the Dorsoduro.

Yet what was worse was his momentary lapse of judgment regarding his professional relationship and responsibility toward Millicent. How quickly he was ready to throw it all away simply for a kiss.

Oh, but what a kiss it would've been.

In his mind's eye Alfredo slowly undressed Millicent, starting with those hideous spectacles of hers and ending with that ridiculous hat she insisted on wearing everywhere and at all times.

Does she actually sleep in her bed at night wearing that cappello idiota?

Yet there was something awfully sweet about that hat. The way it sat on the top of her head, the flower dancing along with her every step. Suddenly he imagined seeing her straddling him as they made love, naked except for the hat, the flower bobbing to and fro with each bounce.

He emitted a throaty giggle. As soon as he did, however, Alfredo whacked his forehead with his fist in an effort to bring himself back to his senses, which wasn't easy to do, now that the crotch of his pants seemed far less roomy than it did seconds earlier.

Ah, Dio in cielo! Why am I thinking of these things? And with Millicent no less? And how could I have allowed her to leave without discussing her fears about going to Nürnberg?

Alfredo decided he must try to catch Millicent before she disappeared completely from view. But it was too late. Holmes, Watson, and Millicent were long gone from the Dorsoduro, and any hope of reaching them now before their departure was impossible. At the very least he had to notify Mr. Smythe and warn him of Millicent's psychiatric fragility.

How could I have been so stupid? And how could I have allowed my beautiful Millicent to travel to the scene of the crime without my professional support and encouragement? Oh, Fredo, Fredo. È stupido, uomo idiota.

Quickly he punched in the number he had done so often in the past regarding Millicent's safety. After two rings he heard the familiar voice of the man who more than once served to allay his fears.

"Smythe here."

✳✳✳

As soon as she opened the door to her hotel suite, Millicent realized she'd little or no time left to pack and get out the door so as to catch her flight to Nürnberg.

"Aunt Kate? Aunt Kate, are you here?" Millicent called out as soon as she and the pugs careened through the open apartment door. "I'm rather pressed for time, and I could desperately use your help."

Still no answer.

Millicent peered into Aunt Kate's bedroom. The room was immaculate. The bed was made and Aunt Kate's clothes were all folded in the bureau drawers or hanging in her closet. Even in the suite, not a single dish was left unwashed or morning coffee remaining in the pot. Nor had she left Millicent a note as to where she'd gone or when she was coming back.

"Oh, bollocks! Why is that woman never here when I need her?" she sputtered *sotto voce*.

Holmes cleared his throat. "I say, Millicent dear, do you still wish for Watson and me to accompany you on your adventure in Nürnberg? I have never been. Have you, Watson?"

"Yeah, never been. I mean, *no*, never been."

It was difficult keeping up with Millicent as she raced from one end of the suite to the other gathering clothes and personal items for her journey. Several times she nearly stepped on top of the anxiously awaiting pugs.

Finally, she stopped, "Well, I suppose so. Yes, good idea as a matter of fact. As far as I know, Mr. Smythe will meet us at the football stadium so I may get a good look at the scene of the crime. I certainly could use your finely honed senses of smell and sight. And besides, it's been far too long since you've had the opportunity to connect with our dear friend Bucky. I know he misses you as you miss him," she announced hurriedly.

As Millicent deftly threw their food dishes, chew toys, and soft bed into an awaiting suitcase, Holmes and Watson danced about her feet. Out of sheer gratitude Watson even jumped up onto her lower legs, his tongue sticking out in rapturous approval.

"Now, boys, you need to stay out of my way as now we've even less time to make our flight than when we'd arrived here." And with that Millicent called for her taxi, sat on each of her three suitcases in order to click and lock them shut, and wrote a quick note to Aunt Kate, letting her know where she and the pugs would be and when they should return.

Meanwhile, Holmes took Watson aside and spoke to him in hushed tones so Millicent wouldn't hear. "Watson, old boy, did you pick up what I did at Doctor Martolini's when that frightening man flew past us?"

"Yeah, flew past us. I recognized 'is scent from the chapel."

"As did I," Holmes said and thoughtfully began to pace. "Something is not quite right at that chapel, and I'm afraid the man at Doctor Martolini's has something to do with it."

"Yeah, to do with it." Watson sat on the side of his right hip and watched Holmes pace back and forth in front of him.

"When we return, you and I shall investigate, dear Watson. In the meantime, we must keep a sharp eye and a keen nose out for Millicent. Something tells me she is in greater danger than we earlier assumed."

"Yeah, danger."

Millicent called for the boys to come. It was time to leave the safety of the Hotel al Ponte Antico and travel toward adventures unknown.

Well, actually Nürnberg.

Chapter 8

Venice, Italy to Nürnberg, Germany

As soon as Millicent along with Holmes and Watson boarded the Bombardier Global 5000 business jet owned and operated by FIFA, she began to worry. It wasn't because Millicent was afraid of flying. She and the pugs had been traversing the skies for well over three years. From their home in Nether Wallop, England to FIFA headquarters in Zurich, Switzerland, and, of course, back again to Doctor Martolini's office in Venice.

Everyone working at the Marco Polo airport knew who she was and took extra special care of her and of her retinue. The pilot usually was Gustav Lindstrom, ex-defender for the Swedish national football team, who now loyally worked for FIFA, flying jets here, there, and everywhere as needed.

No, her fears weren't about the Global 5000 or the blue skies. And as she thought more and more about her anxieties, Millicent realized they were far more complicated than one mere factor could account for. First of all, she was profoundly afraid to retry her hand again at amateur sleuthing, particularly since she'd experienced such an enormous failure on her last assignment.

Millicent lived with her doubts. In fact, she was getting used to doing exactly that. And now with her increasing forgetfulness, she was even more wary of her skills and the burden of responsibility she took on in saving people's lives. Now the entire future of the game of world football (or soccer as Aunt Kate called it) was at stake.

Secondly, she'd never once contemplated attempting such an adventure without first preparing herself under Doctor Martolini's care. Yet the session this morning was anything but reassuring. In fact, it was downright depressing.

How could Alfredo possibly even think of kissing me? And worse yet, how could I have ever attempted to kiss him back?

"Bloody hell," Millicent blurted out loud, causing Holmes and Watson to immediately lift their sleepy heads from the carpeted floor under Millicent's feet. Not wanting to think anymore about Dr. Martolini and his unwarranted behavior, Millicent leaned back into the soft leather business seat and closed her eyes. Soon a slight smile overtook her face. Holmes and Watson seeing such lowered their heads once again onto their front outstretched paws and returned to dozing.

Why shouldn't he kiss me? And why shouldn't I kiss him back? It isn't as if I haven't thought of it before today. In fact, I think about it nearly every day—sometimes three or four times an hour.

It didn't take much time before Millicent was dozing as well. As soon as she began to lightly snore, Holmes opened one eye and set about to garner Watson's attention.

"Psst. I say, Watson, old boy—psst."

Watson let out a wet sigh and twisted himself over onto his left side. Holmes was hesitant to move lest he wake Millicent. He wasn't about to disturb her much-needed sleep. Plus, he desperately needed to speak to Watson before they landed in Nürnberg. And without Millicent's knowledge of their conversation.

Ever so carefully he crawled on his haunches toward Watson a few steps at a time, stopping only to make sure Millicent wasn't disturbed by his movement. Finally, Holmes reached his destination and under the guise of licking the inside of Watson's ear, he instead brought his voice down into a whisper.

"Watson, wake up and be quiet about it. We mustn't awaken Millicent, yet we must talk."

Watson opened one eye and immediately closed it.

"Bethfore shee doeth," he responded with a sleepy slurred lisp.

That did it. Holmes, known for having one of the longest tongues in canine history, unfurled his wet robust muscular hydrostat down Watson's inner ear, tickling the soft cilia of his auditory canal. Watson opened his already wide googly eyes and gave a snort.

"Bloody 'ell," Watson choked out.

"Put a sock in it, old boy. We have to talk, and we have to talk now. If we aren't in agreement before we reach Nürnberg, Millicent could easily be placed in yet another perilous situation, and we both know we can't allow that to happen."

"So, what's the plan?" Watson yawned.

"I'm not sure yet. But when I come up with one, you'll be the first to know."

"'olmes, that man at Dr. Martolini's this morning gave me the collywobbles. I'm not sure I've met 'im before, but I know I didn't like 'im any better this morning than I did then. I think. That is, maybe. I don't know. I'm not sure."

"That's because we haven't already met him, but I smelled something familiar to his scent this morning at the chapel, and that's what has me concerned. I'm not positive, but I think I also smelled another human hiding out in the chapel as well." Holmes did his best detective work while

93

pacing, and that is exactly what he was doing. Meanwhile, Watson had come to a full sitting position.

"You're right. That's why 'e seemed so familiar to me. I don't like 'im or 'is scent one bit. I'm telling you, 'e scares me to death."

Holmes suddenly stopped pacing and stared Watson directly into his googly eyes.

"Well, collywobbles or no collywobbles, we need to find a way to help Millicent with this situation without putting her in any kind of danger. Whatsoever. This is our assignment. And you know better than I, how easy it is for dear Millicent to find her way into dangerous waters."

"Yeah, dangerous waters indeed."

Holmes took in a deep breath and for a few seconds it appeared as if the two pugs had nothing more to say until Watson finally spoke. "So, what's the plan?"

***

As Millicent rested with eyes closed, she could feel the cool evening breeze gently whisking across her face. The gentle whirring of a motor caused her body to tingle and at the same time melt into the chaise where she lay. The slapping of the water against the sides of the boat added to her reverie, and soon she took in the distinct aroma of a lit Galois cigarette.

Wait a minute. I'm aboard an aircraft not a boat. And I don't smoke. And neither does my pilot.

"*Pardonez-moi*, Mademoiselle Winthrop. I hate to disturb you again, but I thought this was as good time as any to speak to you."

Oh, bullocks. It's that bloody tosser of a French detective again.

"You're correct, Mademoiselle. It is I, Inspector General H— pronounced "ahsh"—of the Paris Sûreté at your service. *Enchantez.*" With a slight tilt of his head, the Inspector took her limp hand and lightly kissed the back of it.

"Uh, yes. Of course. Enchantez to you too." Millicent quickly brought her hand up to her lap, not quite sure if she'd been kissed or not.

Oh, crap! Just when I thought I wasn't completely losing my mind. Plus, he's a mind-reader, too.

"I regret to inform you I'm not a mind-reader. But as a purely fictional character I can be whomever the moment requires. And right now it's required I speak to you about the case you're working on before you investigate those at the scene of the crime."

Millicent opened her reluctant eyes, and sure as goodness there he was—that indomitable apparition of her earlier dreams. Not only that, Millicent was no longer on board the Bombardier Global 5000, but on an open-roofed boat, maneuvering its way down the Seine after sunset, and wearing what appeared to be an orange, overstuffed life vest. The street lights from both banks of the river shimmered reflectively on the water below.

What the bloody hell?

"Forgive my intrusion, Mademoiselle. But the flight from Venice to Nürnberg is but a few hours, and I wanted to make sure that not only did you have a restful nap, but that we could take some time to compare notes."

"Sorry?"

"Could I perhaps offer you a cigarette or a croissant?"

Remembering the last time she'd met Monsieur H, Millicent politely declined his kind offer and sat up determined to get her bearings. Quickly she readjusted her hat and skirt.

"Inspector General . . ."

"Monsieur H, please."

"Uh, yes. Monsieur H—'pronounced ahsh,' I know. I must tell you it's highly disconcerting to fall asleep in one place and wake up in quite another. Paris is hardly en route from Venice to Nürnberg. Plus, even though we've already met, I still don't know who the hell you are and why you should suddenly appear to me while I sleep."

The odd little Frenchman took one last drag of his cigarette before flicking it over the side of the boat. With gentle eyes and a warm smile he turned his attention to Millicent.

"*Ma chérie*, Millicent. I'm always available to you for consultation and perhaps a partnership in your crime solving. But I can only come to you in your dream life. After all, my mere existence is only in a few novels and your imagination. And since you haven't had time lately to read, *voila*. Here I am."

For some odd reason that seemed to make sense to Millicent. Plus, it was true. She could use whatever help she could get. Aunt Kate was never around, Dr. Martolini was either too busy or too distracted to pay attention to her needs, and Mr. Smythe was confined to Zurich. Her only resources were Holmes and Watson, and they were pugs, not seasoned professional sleuths.

"Very well then. I appreciate your attention and desire to assist me in this troubling case."

"*Il me fait plaisir*, Mademoiselle Millicent. Now please tell me, what do you hope to find in Nürnberg? You're going to the scene of the crime, *n'est pas?*"

"*Absolutement.* Of course," Millicent answered, not quite sure why she was beginning to speak in French.

What in the bloody hell's going on?

"Once again I beg your indulgence. If you begin to speak in French, it's perhaps because I wish you to. After all, our conversation is as much my dream as it's yours." Monsieur H grinned from ear to ear, enjoying no end his wit at her expense.

Like any good detective Inspector H was a bit of a trickster himself.

He wondered in what ways Millicent may be one as well. It's always wise for a good detective to have a secret weapon and a trick or two up his or her sleeve. One never knew when something like that could come in handy.

"*Je vous demande pardon*, Mademoiselle. I beg your forgiveness. I feel somewhat frisky today due to your connection with this new case. It's been a long time since I've had the opportunity to assist someone as capable and captivating as yourself, *ma chérie*."

Millicent felt herself blush, but she kept focused on the reassuring eyes of her new friend.

"So kind of you to say so. I'm humbled by your professional opinion, Monsieur. As to the scene of the crime, I plan on visiting the team locker room as soon as I arrive. Mr. Smythe as well as the Nürnberg *polizei* promised to be there to guide me through the few clues gathered and what still remains missing in their investigation. Also, my colleagues Holmes and Watson will be with me, and if any two assistants can find obscure clues, they can."

Mon Dieu. She actually believes her sweet petite chiens can help her solve this crime. I have my work cut out for me. Assurément, thought Monsieur H.

"It has been my experience, Mademoiselle, if at all possible, our victim . . ."

"Riccardo Stillitano."

"*Oui*, Riccardo Stillitano, our victim would've put up a fight or left some kind of clue if he could. He's an athlete, after all, and perhaps would have been strong enough to put up quite a struggle before his abductor killed him or stole him away." The detective took out a miniature notebook out of his vest pocket and with a pen began to list a few of his thoughts.

"I'm told by my superior at FIFA the German police have thoroughly gone over the locker room. They found no fingerprints, no evidence of a weapon, and no blood spatter whatsoever." Millicent was already beginning to feel the hopelessness of solving the case and sighed.

"Ah, but Mademoiselle, this is a good sign. Tell me, how many men's locker rooms can you think of in professional football that would be entirely clean of fingerprints or blood for that matter—particularly while a game goes on at the same time? No, our criminal made sure he cleaned up after himself, which leads me to believe he didn't act alone." Monsieur H made yet another note to himself.

"So what you're saying Inspector is there still may be evidence in the locker room, evidence which can't be seen by the naked eye?" Millicent stood up from the chaise and began to pace from one side of the boat to the other, wobbling as best she could in an effort to find her sea legs.

"*Exactement*," Monsieur H said excitedly.

Suddenly Millicent felt the boat lurch, forcing her to career across the stern and nearly tumble over the side of the boat. As she grabbed onto the rail, she could feel her life vest begin to vibrate and the water of the Seine caress her face as she hung on for dear life. Then she heard what sounded like the voice of her pilot Gustav speaking over the intercom.

"Millicent, this is Captain Lindstrom. As you can probably already tell, we're experiencing some heavy turbulence as we make our descent into Nürnberg. I've turned on this seatbelt sign for your safety. Perhaps you should kennel Holmes and Watson as well. We will be on the ground in but a few minutes."

"Huh?" Millicent woke with a start.

Now where am I? And what's Holmes doing on my lap licking my face? Incroyable.

Now fully awake Millicent led Holmes, who did indeed happen to be on her lap, followed by Watson into a secured kennel, and then made her own way to her seat. As she was buckling herself in, she glanced down at the table in front of her, her eyes latching onto a tiny piece of notebook paper with a To Do list written in impeccable French.

Well, how do you like that?

***

Nürnberg, Germany

By the time Millicent and the pugs reached the Nürnberg Grundig-Stadion locker room, Mr. Smythe was already conferring with the two local city detectives in charge of the case.

"Gentlemen, I wish to commend you on the fine job you've done in assessing the crime scene. We at FIFA appreciate your thoroughness and your skill. However, as indicated in my email, one of our own special liaisons with the Security Council should arrive momentarily to see if anything may've been missed."

Mr. Smythe was always exceptionally careful in the way he dealt with other police entities. It wouldn't look good on FIFA's image should a country feel slighted or humiliated, particularly on matters which dealt with crimes against footballers.

The younger of the two German detectives glanced back at his superior and began to fidget. Obviously, he'd been taken aback by Mr. Smythe's heeding, and probably for no other reason than he was new to these procedures. The older detective, sensing his colleague's frustration, put his hand reassuringly on the younger man's shoulder before turning back at Mr. Smythe.

"We here in Nürnberg understand, Herr Smythe, the gravity of this situation and promise to fully cooperate. It's as important to us as it is to you to follow appropriate procedures. If anything is further needed, our department will only be too glad to assist your liaison—"

Suddenly in mid sentence, Millicent, followed nervously by Holmes and Watson, burst through the double locker room doors—the dogs barking madly. Once again Millicent could barely control the enthusiastic demonstration by her two eager friends.

As she released their leads, Holmes and Watson set out sniffing the entire locker room from one end to the other. Disheveled as usual, Millicent quickly gave her attention to re-tucking her blouse, capturing her stray wisps of hair back into their mandatory bun, and adjusting her crumpled hat from leaning too far askew with its wilted decorative flower looking at if it had endured a typhoon.

"Halt! No one's allowed in here!" cried the young detective as he moved anxiously to retrieve his holstered gun. Immediately, the older detective assessed the situation, noticed Mr. Smythe smiled at the unwarranted guests, and so turned to his younger partner.

"It's all right, Fritz. I believe Mr. Smythe's familiar with our visitors."

Mr. Smythe chuckled respectfully. "Gentlemen, allow me to introduce Millicent Winthrop, special liaison to the Security Council of the Fédération Internationale de Football Association, and her two assistants, Holmes and Watson."

"*Gott in Himmel,* Wolfgang. This goes beyond appropriate procedures."

Wolfgang Sanders, the older of the two detectives, burst into a hardy laugh. "You've much to learn, Fritz. But in the meantime we mustn't forget our manners. It's my greatest pleasure to make your acquaintance, Frau Winthrop," he said, offering his hand.

"Fräulein, actually." Millicent noted the detective's yellowed teeth as she shook his hand.

I wonder if he smokes Galois as well.

She then offered her hand to Fritz Reitmeyer. The young man couldn't help but roll his eyes as he extended his hand to her in return. "Fräulein Winthrop."

"Millicent, please." Millicent presented her most socially-practiced smile. "I apologize for our bold entrance, but it's obvious my partners have picked up something important, perhaps the scent of our kidnapper."

Mr. Smythe took up the conversation. "Don't be deceived by Millicent's unorthodox manner. Believe me, gentlemen, it took us at the Security Council several months to respect and appreciate her extraordinary talents and skills as a sleuth. Her eccentricities may make her at times appear inconsequential, but rest assured, *she* is not."

Detective Sanders graciously nodded. "Detective Reitmeyer and I, Detective Sanders, welcome you to Nürnberg, Fräulein. As I reminded Mr. Smythe earlier, we're here to serve you—all four of you—in any way we can."

In that moment Millicent remembered the conversation she'd had with Monsieur H not more than an hour earlier. Intimidated by the younger detective but welcomed by the elder, Millicent drew upon her courage.

"I do have one question, detectives. Your initial report failed to mention if any blood residue or fingerprints were found here at the scene of the crime. Was that true or merely an oversight in your statement?"

Detective Reitmeyer began to noticeably seethe. "It wasn't an oversight, Fräulein Winthrop." His words hissed through his clenched teeth.

"Millicent, actually," she continued. "Not for a moment did I think it was, Herr Detective. I simply find it odd that in a locker room filled with a team of bloodied, ungloved players—save for the goalkeeper—not a single droplet of blood or fingerprint partial emerged. Does that not seem unusual to you?"

Detective Sanders face took on a serious demeanor. "You're absolutely correct, Fräulein. We hadn't thought of that."

"I take it you didn't use forensic luminol in your investigation." Mr. Smythe jumped in knowing Millicent wouldn't be as aware as he of current investigation procedures. In the meantime Holmes and Watson had meandered back to their mistress and plopped themselves obediently at her feet.

Wolfgang Sanders again answered for both detectives. "*Es tut uns leid.* We're indeed very sorry, but we did not. It's obvious now to us whoever abducted Herr Stillitano cleaned away all evidence. If you would like, we will continue our assessment of the locker room and send you our report immediately."

Holmes and Watson barked in approval. "Well, Millicent," interjected

Mr. Smythe, "does that meet with your approval?"

Millicent smiled confidently. "Thank you, gentlemen. We must all work together in order to solve the case as quickly as humanly possible. A young man's life is possibly at stake. I needn't say more."

Suddenly, as if out of nowhere Millicent's body began to tremble. At first no one seemed to notice, thinking she was merely cold for the locker room was damp from the moisture-laden weather. But when Mr. Smythe saw Millicent's flower rhythmically bob from left to right, he immediately realized she was having one of her visions.

And he wasn't the only one. Soon Holmes and Watson were barking and jumping up on Millicent's lower legs. Mr. Smythe had no other recourse but to stare at Millicent as her eyes rolled toward the back of her head.

"*Ach du liebe,*" voiced Detective Sanders. "Has Fräulein Winthrop taken ill?"

Both Detective Sanders and Detective Reitmeyer rushed to Millicent's aid. To the young detective's chagrin Millicent wilted like a ragdoll into his arms. The three gentlemen placed Millicent gently on the floor where she shook and moaned for what seemed an eternity. Finally, she opened her eyes wide.

"Oh bugger!" And with that retort Millicent was out like a light.

Holmes and Watson stood guard while Millicent lay in her semi-comatose state, Holmes at her head and Watson at her feet. Mr. Smythe knew from past experience Millicent would be all right once the vision had passed. Holmes and Watson were privy to it as well, but that knowledge didn't keep them from maintaining their vigil.

"As I said earlier," Mr. Smythe began, "Millicent has a rather unconventional approach to crime solving. Because of her brain injury three years ago she has been both blessed and cursed with some astounding skills and talents, none of which I've ever experienced before."

"But why is she lying there on the floor?" questioned Detective Reitmeyer. "It doesn't look to me like she's doing much of anything except perhaps taking a nap."

It was obvious to Mr. Smythe that Detective Sanders was becoming more and more frustrated with his young partner. "Fritz, I've learned many things over the years but one of the most important has been to always keep an open mind. As soon as you close yourself off to any and all resources, you're doing a disservice to not only you but to the solving of the crime as well."

Detective Sanders took a moment to regroup. Another tactic was obviously needed. "You're too good of a detective to be so narrow minded and faultfinding. We may have some things to learn from this young lady. Things you and I may not be accustomed to or feel comfortable with, but things we must make ourselves available to nonetheless."

"Ja, Wolfgang. Du bist recht." The young detective knew in his heart his mentor was correct, but this was ridiculous.

Millicent gave a snort and promptly turned herself over onto her stomach, arms and legs stretched out in all directions. If it wasn't for the fact she was snoring, one would believe she'd returned to the coma she'd initially been in those three years ago. Holmes and Watson decided to follow suit.

Holmes cuddled up to her right side and Watson to her left. Then they too began to snore. Millicent may have appeared like a ragdoll floating in a puddle of sleep, but she was anything but. She was having one of her so-called episodes, even if she didn't recognize this herself. But Mr. Smythe, along with Holmes and Watson most certainly did.

***

In her mind Millicent was still in the locker room, yet now alone, getting ready to kidnap her victim as soon as she could knock him out. Quickly she opened the bottle of chloroform, keeping it at a distance so as not to fall victim to her evil intentions. She could feel both anger and elation as she waited for the young midfielder to open the door to his doom.

She wanted to laugh but quickly silenced herself and her assistant so as not to be made by Riccardo Stillitano, star player for FC Nürnberg. She had nothing personally against him—he was merely a pawn in her scheme to get back at those who had harmed her and her family so many years ago.

This is for you, Katya. And for you, too, mama and papa. Everyone will be made sorry for what happened to you, and they will pay heavily. This I promise you. As long as I have breath, I will take my revenge.

Millicent then heard footsteps approaching the locker room. Quickly she lifted the phone receiver off the wall and hid herself behind the door. As the Italian soccer star entered hurriedly toward the phone, she just as swiftly jumped on his back and held the drenched cloth up against his face. Stillitano fought for his life—grabbing at her hands, trying to remove them from his mouth and nose. But it was all too much and soon he fell lifelessly to the floor.

You're not dead yet, my friend. Just like your people tortured my sister, I will make sure your painful death will be excruciatingly slow.

Millicent then motioned for her assistant to help carry the sleeping midfielder to a closely parked van, which in turn transported the three of them to an awaiting speedboat moored on the Pegnitz River.

***

As rapidly as Millicent had passed out, she suddenly came to.

"So sorry gentlemen to have given a scare, but when these occasions loom up, I've no other recourse but to surrender. I believe I now have a strong idea as to how this crime occurred. Allow me please to explain."

Mr. Smythe assisted Millicent to her feet. "Millicent, dear girl, I forgot to tell you that Dr. Martolini called right after your session with him this morning," he said quietly in her ear. "He's extremely concerned and feels badly he was unable to give you the full attention you needed before flying here this morning. I believe it will be important for you to touch base with him when you return to Venice. Will you promise me you will call him as soon as you land?"

Mr. Smythe knew after one of her episodes Millicent could sometimes become psychologically and emotionally fragile. It would be important for her to see Alfredo as soon as she was able.

"Huh? Oh, yes. Of course, Dr. Martolini. Humpf!" she said, but then proceeded to describe her vision and in some detail. When she finished, Millicent merely re-straightened her glasses, her hair and her hat, grabbed the dogs' leashes, and with a shy smile bid the three men, "*Grüss Gott.*"

Along with Holmes and Watson she then left the locker room and quickly took her seat in a special box provided by the Nürnberg football club. The afternoon match was about to start, and Millicent and her retinue refused to miss a single moment of this important game between the home club and that of Borussia Dortmund. With her pint-sized glass of Pilsner in hand, Millicent sat back to enjoy the reward of her day's labor, proud of all she'd accomplished and in such a short amount of time.

Chapter 9

Zurich, Switzerland

Mr. Smythe took up the white starched napkin from his lap and thoroughly wiped his mouth clean. Sabrina always prepared the finest of dinners, particularly when he had to travel out of the country, for that meant he had put in a profitable and possibly hectic day. She usually chose dishes taught to her by her German mother.

Bucky's favorite was a meal made up of *Jaegerschnitzel* (pork cutlet with mushroom gravy), *rotkraut* (red cabbage) and *Spaetzle* (German egg noodles). And true to form, this is precisely what Sabrina served her hard-working husband to his sheer and over-satiated delight.

"Can I get you anything else, Bucky dear?" Sabrina asked her husband as he pushed his chair away from the table and leaned back. "A tea or a coffee perhaps?" Sabrina stood up to take the dirty dishes back into the kitchen.

"Yes, my dear. A cup of tea would be wonderful. Thank you." Mr. Smythe and his wife had been married for many years, but in all that time they never were blessed to have had a child. Instead, Bucky and Sabrina tended to take on lost people or strays, if you will. And Millicent fit that bill to a tee.

No one knew exactly Millicent's background or how it was she found herself at the hospital for amnesiac disorders in London. How old was she? Was she married? Were her parents still alive? One thing was for certain— no one was looking for Millicent. And she did after all have Aunt Kate to look after her. Nonetheless, both Sabrina and her husband had a special place in their hearts for the sweet, talented but shy Millicent Winthrop.

"So are you going to finally tell me how your day went with Millicent, or am I going to have to pour this tea over your head?" Sabrina loved to tease her husband, and no matter how tired or busy he was, Bucky always found a way to enjoy her soft but unrelenting banter. She placed two teacups and the tea cozy onto the table.

"That will hardly be necessary, Rina," he said laughingly. "Our little Millicent becomes more and more adroit in her detecting skills with each passing day. But I do worry about her. These trances she often finds herself in are taking their toll on her health, I'm afraid. I doubt she sleeps worth a nickel, and to me she appears to be getting thinner and thinner. I know the work's getting to her—that's apparent. But she's our only hope in tracking down this fiend and bringing him to justice."

Sabrina, now seated at the table opposite him, placed her hands lovingly on top of her husband's. "You shouldn't feel guilty, my dear. Millicent's stronger than you think. I'm sure of it. And besides, Doctor Martolini is keeping a close eye on her progress, even as we speak. He's extremely knowledgeable and he cares about her very much."

Bucky let out a deep sigh. "I suppose you're right. Alfredo's a fine psychiatrist, there's no denying that. And I can't say enough about the love, intelligence, and loyalty Holmes and Watson demonstrate toward our dear Millicent. They never leave her side, no matter what."

"Then let's not worry needlessly about our Millicent. I promise you she's in safe hands." Sabrina smiled tenderly. "Or in the Holmes's and Watson's case, paws. Come, let's finish our tea and then go to bed. You must be tired, and I need to sleep in the sweet safety of your love tonight."

She stood as she winked at her husband and took him by the hand. She then led him away from the table and down the hall to their bedroom, all the way smiling demurely. The old friends completely forgot about their tea. For as soon as the door shut, they fell into each other's arms.

***

Venice, Italy

Alfredo Martolini couldn't get a single thing done that day. Instead he decided to cancel his afternoon appointments and take a short walk to the market to shop for his evening meal.

His concerns regarding Millicent had been somewhat assuaged after his morning phone conversation with Mr. Smythe. Yet Alfredo still couldn't shake the feeling that Millicent was in some kind of trouble. He searched his memory and still couldn't recollect when Millicent had appeared quite as vulnerable as she had that morning.

Dammit. Mannaggia a me. What's the matter with me? I swear, I'm losing it over this silly woman and her little pugs—i suoi piccolo Carlini. Oh, Alfredo. Alfredo. What have you done?

The doctor moved through the market as if in a daze. He sauntered past his favorite stand of fresh crab, sardines, and turbot with disinterest. Even the vegetable vendors with their fennel, chard, and broccolini failed to appeal.

Dio mio. Now I'm not only losing my mind, but my appetite too.

Not wanting to return home empty-handed, he went ahead and purchased several slices of prosciutto and fresh melon for his mamma along with his favorite bottle of pinot grigio, *Di Lenardo* 2012. If he wasn't able to eat, he could at the very least get drunk.

As soon as Alfredo reached his door, he heard his office phone ring. Thinking it might be Millicent, he tore up the stairs as fast as his feet could take him.

"*Pronto?*"

"*Dobar dan, doktor.* Good afternoon. I hope I'm not interrupting you." Surprised it wasn't Millicent on the other end of the line, it took Alfredo several seconds to recognize the man's voice.

"*Sì*, this is Doctor Martolini. And, no, you're not interrupting me."

"Good. Good. I wish to apologize for my abrupt manner this morning. I wasn't my usual self, *doktor*, and I wanted to call and invite you to dinner this evening as a way of making up for my inappropriate behavior."

Alfredo was now certain this was the man who had charged erratically around his office that morning. "I assure you, signore. Your actions weren't unusual for a man who has gone through as much heartbreak as you have. There's nothing to forgive, trust me. I thank you deeply for the invitation, but I feel I must refuse." Alfredo didn't for a second believe his rebuttal would be accepted, but it was worth a try nonetheless.

"Nonsense. I'm a rude bastard, I know. But what I put you through this morning was unforgivable. So, let us meet, say, nine o'clock for a late dinner and a few drinks? Will the Bàcaro Jazz work for you? It's located near the *Ponte di Rialto*."

Alfredo somehow knew the insistent man wasn't likely to let up until he gave in. *Mamma mia.*

"*Sì*, of course. I won't be able to stay out late, but I will join you tonight for a light dinner and perhaps a Sambuca."

"*Divan*. Wonderful, *doktor*. Then I will see you there."

The phone went dead before anything else could be said. Alfredo wasn't particularly interested in meeting anyone this evening, with the exception of Millicent, of course. Yet there was something compelling about this strange man. Being a psychiatrist, Alfredo couldn't help but be fascinated with the possibility of helping this foreigner come to terms with his grief and anger. Yet as a man he sensed he may be walking into an extremely dangerous trap.

***

Alfredo arrived at the Jazz Club slightly before eight o'clock that evening. He was dressed informally, even though the cool night air required he wear one of his warmer jackets. These October days were still warm in Venice, but the evenings brought cooler winds across the Adriatic and into the city proper.

Alfredo had barely hung up his coat when he saw the man sitting by himself at a nearby table for two. He, too, had changed clothes from this morning's rumpled suit and looked quite comfortable in his blue cashmere V-neck sweater and dark brown chinos. Alfredo thought to himself that had the man not made this appointment with him earlier that day, he wouldn't have recognized him to be the same person.

"*Kado si, doktor*? How are you?" The man stood up from where he sat and motioned Alfredo to his table.

"Good, *bene*. This is a lovely bistro. It's been some time since I've dined here."

"I know. I dine here often and haven't seen you before tonight, *Doktor* Martolini." The two men shook hands.

"Alfredo, please. *Per favore.*"

"Alfredo it is." The man smiled and stared intently into the doctor's eyes. He had the most unusual smile, thought Alfredo. It was as if from the nose up he was frowning, but from the upper lip down he wore a feeble grin.

"And you are . . . ?"

The man didn't immediately answer. Finally he took in a deep breath and said simply, "You may call me Nik—short for Osvetnik. It's a name I've always tried to live up to."

"A family name?"

"You could say that."

The two men were interrupted by the waiter arriving with their food. "I hope you don't mind, Alfredo, but I took it upon myself to order for both of us. My stomach's temperamental these days. Very few foods agree with me, you understand."

Alfredo came to the realization that this evening could go one of two ways. The two men would either develop a fine comradeship, or they would become mortal enemies.

He glanced at the food plate before him and decided perhaps there might be a chance the two men could somehow connect with each other in spite of the bizarre set of circumstances.

"And because we're having fish I thought it would be appropriate to also order a bottle of pinot grigio. I hope that agrees with you?" Nik asked but waited for an answer. After the waiter pulled the cork, Nik poured the wine first into the doctor's glass and then into his own. Placing the bottle in the center of the table, he then raised his glass.

"To a new friendship. May it last longer than my days on this earth."

"Sì, Nik, to friendship." The two men clanked their glasses together before setting out to enjoy their meal.

***

The evening continued without a hitch. The two men talked about everything from current Venetian politics to Alfredo's work with amnesiacs. And Nik's love of American whiskey. Finally, the discussion turned to what both men seemed to have most in common—the lack of a woman's love in their lives.

"So, you're not married, is that so, Alfredo?"

"True, I'm unmarried. Unfortunately, I've known very few women whom I felt I could fall in love with."

"But you're such a . . . , how do the American's say, 'a good-catch', yes?"

"You mean, because I'm a psychiatrist?"

Nik chuckled. "Yes. That and you're good looking, wealthy, and Italian. What more could any woman want?"

Alfredo wanted to laugh but he couldn't. "Yes, 'what more', as you say. But perhaps a woman wants a man not married to his job, for one thing," he continued. "And not committed to taking care of his aging mother, for another. These two things have in the past been obstacles to nearly every relationship I've been in."

"Ah, so family's important to you?"

"*Molto*. I often think I'd like to have children of my own someday, but *someday* never seems to come. And how about you? Do you have a woman? Children?"

Nik's demeanor turned dark. "No, no. The world's much too evil to bring a child into. I wouldn't want anyone to experience what I went through as a boy. Besides, very few women are interested in falling in love with a man like me—emotionally inaccessible, tortured, and bordering on insane." He then smiled, but only his mouth showed any glimpse of cordiality. His eyes were as cold as glass.

"Don't you think a good woman would be able to see through your pain and love you for who you truly are?"

The man leaned forward and directed his steel gaze directly into Alfredo's eyes. "I'm a dangerous person, Dr. Martolini. Don't be fooled by my hospitality. If you were my enemy, I wouldn't hesitate this very moment to slit your throat right where you sit."

He then leaned back in his chair, his face suddenly reverting to a socially warm and cheerful façade. "But, of course, we aren't talking about you, are we? Women are the topic, yes? Women and love, whatever that means."

Alfredo felt the hair on the back of his neck stand up. The mercurial nature of this man at once both fascinated and terrified him. His curiosity begged him to stay at the bistro a bit longer, but his good sense told him it was time to leave before the conversation escalated and Nik once again became volatile.

"I'm anything but your enemy, Nik. It would be an honor to be your therapist, and a great privilege to be your friend." Alfredo then stood up from his chair. "I want to thank you for this lovely evening. It wasn't necessary, but greatly enjoyed nonetheless. I must get home as I've a day filled with clients tomorrow, and mamma will be wondering where I've gone off to."

Nik stood to shake the doctor's hand and was about to say he would get in touch with him soon, when a startlingly beautiful woman strode into the club. And apparently all by herself. Both men stared at the great beauty, their mouths agape. The woman found her way to the bar and sat on one of the modern-designed leather bar stools.

Her long straight hair was dark brown, nearly black, with a shock of white extending from the left side of the top of her head to just below her shoulder blades. Her eyes were dark blue, almost violet, and her flawless skin was translucent alabaster. Her midnight blue dress clung to her shapely body. It was cut with a high bodice in front but with a plunging slit on the flipside exposing her well-toned back.

She obviously wasn't wearing a bra or anything else underneath, for that matter. An additional slit up her left leg allowed the beauty to gracefully slip up onto the barstool without tearing her dress or hiking it above the standards of elegance and propriety. Both men immediately registered that this woman was pure class.

Nik was the first to let go of Alfredo's handshake, his eyes still on the woman ahead. No sooner had the woman sat, than Nik made his way over to the bar.

"Pardon me, beautiful lady. I couldn't help but notice you're by yourself this evening. Are you waiting for someone? Or would you give my friend, Dr. Martolini, and me the honor of your presence at our table? I assure you, we mean you every courtesy."

The woman peered up at him with curtained eyes. "I am sorry. Do I know you, monsieur?"

Her French accent was subtle but nonetheless noticeable.

"Not yet, mademoiselle. But I doubt you will be disappointed in our company. Alfredo and I are the most interesting men in all of Venice, and you're obviously the most stunning woman in the entire city. So, we were meant for each other, *n'est pas*?"

The woman glanced past Nik at the gentleman standing near the table and gave a slight smile and nod of her head. She then stared directly into Nik's eyes. His breath hitched.

"Perhaps I will join you for a short time," she said as she smiled. "I am supposed to meet someone here tonight, but you drive a hard bargain, Monsieur . . . ?"

"Please, call me Nik." He took the woman's hand and assisted her to her feet. He then placed his other hand on the bare skin of her back and led her to the table where Alfredo still stood with his mouth half-open.

"Mademoiselle, allow me to introduce my serious friend, Dr. Alfredo Martolini."

"Enchantez, mademoiselle. Alfredo, please." Alfredo was so mesmerized, he wasn't aware he'd spoken, even though he thought he heard a few words leave his mouth. He kissed the back of the woman's free hand while Nik seated her in the chair between them.

"And please call me Veronica. Veronica Nero."

"Veronica Nero," both men answered simultaneously as she smiled gracefully. It was obvious to Nik that Alfredo was smitten, and equally obvious to Alfredo that Nik was likewise besotted. This also didn't go

121

unnoticed by the mysterious beauty sharing the table with them.

After an uncomfortable pause Alfredo decided to stimulate some conversation. "May we get you something to drink, Mademoiselle Nero?"

"It's Veronica. And please, I'll take a Balcone's Fifth Anniversary Whiskey on the rocks."

Nik's eyes widened. "So, you're an American whiskey drinker as well?"

"*Oui.* I usually prefer Tennessee whiskeys, but this one from Texas is a true gem."

Nik motioned for the waiter to return to their table.

Alfredo began to chuckle. "And how do you come to know so much about whiskey, Veronica?"

"My mother was an American and very much a connoisseur of the beverage, if you know what I mean." Her face grew serious for a brief moment, and then her inviting smile returned.

Soon Alfredo began to feel like the odd man out. No matter how often he attempted to attract Veronica's attention, she appeared to only be interested in his new friend.

And Nik couldn't keep his eyes off of her. Alfredo once again was about to excuse himself when Nik asked Veronica the question both men were craving to know. "So, this person you're meeting here tonight, is it a man?"

"*Oui,*" she answered without hesitation.

Nik persisted in his questioning. "And is this man your husband or your lover?"

Just then, the waiter had returned with the whiskey Nik had ordered.

Veronica smiled. "Monsieur, you cannot ask a woman that kind of question in front of three handsome men. And even if I could answer you, which I won't, why would you even believe a single thing I said?"

Nik's eyes creased to match his arresting smile. "Touché, Veronica. Touché."

He then lifted his drink to hers and clinked her glass. Alfredo, although entranced by both the beauty and mystery of the woman next to him, again decided that it was probably time to get back home.

He stood to his feet. "Nik, it's been a delight, but I must be going. And Veronica, it was lovely to have spent the evening with you as well. Hopefully, we will meet again."

"*Mais, bien sûr*, Alfredo. But, of course. *Ciao*."

She offered the doctor her hand, which he thought twice about kissing, and so politely held it briefly in his own. Alfredo then exited the club and strolled toward home.

It was a lovely evening, with barely a nip of autumn in the air. Soon his thoughts returned to Millicent's safety and welfare. Like the woman he met tonight, Millicent was altogether enchanting. Her softness, her vulnerabilities, her quirkiness, her genius—everything about her enthralled him.

Something else about Veronica also reminded Alfredo of Millicent, but what it was he couldn't quite put his finger on. The woman at first meeting appeared to be sophisticated, Millicent was anything but. Veronica was seductive, Millicent, although fascinating, compared to Veronica wasn't even close to what one would call *a siren*.

Their accents, their apparel, their sense of self—the two women were as far from each other as could possibly be imagined. And yet something about Veronica's smile compelled the good doctor to imagine his lips taking advantage of Millicent's.

"*Buon dio in cielo*. Good God in Heaven, Alfredo. You must be losing your mind," he heard himself speak out loud as he made his way across the Accademia Bridge. Alfredo convinced himself he only thought these things because it was late, he was tired, and he quite possibly had had too much to drink.

Why else would he be torturing himself with all these niggling thoughts? Yet he worried about Millicent more than he wanted to admit.

As he opened the door to his home, Alfredo promised himself to call Millicent first thing in the morning. By then she should be home from her duties in Nürnberg and ready to reschedule her next session.

***

Veronica continued to nurse her drink, taking only occasional sips of the potent liquid. Nik, on the other hand, was enjoying himself far too much. Four drinks earlier he'd switched his cocktail to the same whiskey as hers. The faster he talked, the more he drank, and the more he drank, the more inebriated he became.

Everything about the man was big—his laugh, his stories, his gestures, and his flirting. Veronica did her best to respond in her own quiet way. She smiled at his jokes, nodded her head in agreement to his odd opinions, and took in the tales about his life with the empathetic skill of an attentive listener. Finally, as if he had run out of gas, Nik excused himself.

As he weaved his way to the men's room, Veronica reached inside her purse for a tiny vial of liquid, which she then poured into the remaining whiskey left in Nik's glass. She had a mission to accomplish this evening, and she needed to make sure Nik wouldn't impede her in any way. Veronica gave the drink a swirl with her finger, and then added what alcohol remained in her own drink to the concoction. She was drying her fingers with her cloth napkin when Nik returned to his seat.

"I don't wish for this evening to end, Veronica. You're a woman a man such as me could only dream of being with. Yet here you are, and here I'm at your mercy," he said, leaning forward in his chair. Taking her hands in his, Nik pressed wet kisses to her palms. Veronica let out a tiny gasp in response. This was going to be more difficult than she had earlier thought.

"Please, *ma chérie*. Come home with me tonight and let me show you my appreciation for your kind attention to one such as me. It's been a long time since I've been with a woman as beautiful as you. I would consider it a great honor if you would share my bed."

Veronica lowered her eyelids and spoke as seductively as the noisy jazz club would allow. "Finish your drink first while I think about it."

Nik chugged what was left in his drink in two large gulps. Veronica then gazed into his eyes filled with smoky desire and smiled coyly. "I'm all yours," she said with such intensity Nik nearly fell out of his chair. Instead, he pulled a wad of money out of his pocket and lay what was needed for the bill on the table.

"I live not far from here. Let me assist you with your wrap." The two of them stood at once. Veronica watched as the light-headed Nik grabbed the table to keep from falling. "It seems I've had a bit more to drink than usual. But fear not, *mom amour*, I won't let you down."

Lurching forward, Nik reached for Veronica and pulled her into his swarthy arms. He then kissed her with as much bravado as he could muster without losing his balance. When he let her go, his eyes betrayed a man desperate to find some fragment of love and tenderness no matter how fleeting—a shard of hope to bring light to his everyday world of brutality and pain. In that moment the man seemed more fragile than dangerous, and so Veronica got her things and went with him out into the starlit night, linking her arm in his as he led her through the streets of

126

Venice to his apartment.

Chapter 10

Nik could hardly keep his eyes open let alone stay upright on his feet. And just his luck, too. Here he was arm-in-arm with the outrageously scrumptious Veronica, possibly the sexiest woman in the entire world, and he couldn't see straight.

It took all his effort simply to put one foot in front of the other. Veronica, however, didn't seem to mind him leaning into her soft curvaceous body, forcing him to stay as perpendicular to the piazza as he could manage.

Luckily Nik was at least able to remember where he lived and how to get there. He could do it with his eyes closed, which was pretty much where he now was at. Venice had a particularly romantic aura about it when one's eyes were blurred. As drunk as he was, Nik still took advantage of his surroundings and muzzled his cheek against Veronica's bare neck.

When the two finally arrived, Veronica was astonished to find she recognized the familiar building. In fact, nearly everyone in Venice, resident and tourist alike, knew of this beautiful but rundown edifice. Nik took her in through the back and up a flight of stairs to his apartment, such as it was.

Basically the studio was nothing more than a loft. One oversized room made all the more vacuous by its lack of furniture. Two mismatched kitchen chairs bookended a long coffee table covered with newspapers, magazines and unopened mail.

A stool positioned itself against a counter close to the makeshift kitchen, and, surprise . . . surprise, the man didn't even own a sofa. Nik was by this time weaving in and out of consciousness, so Veronica had no other choice but to unload him onto his ample bed. She was about to walk away, when he grasped her by the wrist.

"And where do you think you're going, *moja lijepa jedan*, my beauty?" Nik slurred.

Interesting language. Slavic, perhaps?

"I am right here, Nik. I was about to take your shoes off so you would be more comfortable, *n'est pas?*"

"I'd best be most comfortable if both of us took our clothes off." He smiled at her, his eyes rolling back into his head.

Veronica needed to stall. She'd promised to do a thorough check of the

129

old building before leaving, but she couldn't do that until this ridiculous man was completely out.

"You must know I am a bit shy, Nik. Perhaps you have something here we could drink? Another whiskey perhaps?" She threw one of her coquettish smiles his way. Nik held his breath and then grinned even broader in return.

"Oh, I understand you now. You want to party with your new friend, Nik, huh?" he hiccupped. "Look in the cupboard above the sink. That's where I keep my special reserve."

He hiccupped again.

"Have you ever tried Rakia, *moja lijepa jedan*? It's probably the only sweet thing to have ever come out of my sad country," he laughed, but Veronica heard the bitterness beneath his words.

Nik let go of Veronica's wrist, fell back into his bed and started to sing. Keeping beat with his fist thumping his chest, Nik released the saddest melody Veronica had ever heard. His words held so much fervor that for a moment Veronica was momentarily stopped from removing his obstinate shoes, which felt as if they were cemented onto his feet.

Instead, she stared at him. What happened next took Nik by as much surprise as it did Veronica. He wept. And not only a few measly tears. Nik let the dam break, wailing at the top of his voice, encouraged no doubt by his rendition of whatever the words were to the song he sang.

130

"Please, Veronica. *Molim te.* Hold me. Come lay next to me and hold me."

Something inside Veronica's head told her to get the hell out of that room and get on with her assignment, but she didn't have it within her heart to ignore the poor man. So she did the unforgivable. The thing most forbidden in the book of political espionage. She slipped off her shoes along with her dress and lay next to the emotionally besotted Nik, whose arms encircled her for fear of letting go.

"Shhh, Nik. Go to sleep. It's all right. I am here," Veronica repeated as she stroked his out-of-place hair from off his forehead. This went on for what felt like hours, but in next to no time his grip loosened and his snoring took over the room. Veronica now had no choice but to slip out of his bed and get on with her search.

Carefully she lifted the arm which had wrapped itself around her and placed it on the pillow she'd wedged next to him, hoping that should he awaken, he would think she was still in his arms. She then slid down to the floor, one inch at a time, until she was on all fours. She was ready to crawl across the floor and retrieve her dress, jacket and shoes, when she heard Nik drowsily speak.

She froze where she was until she realized he must be dreaming. The angry foreign words he spoke weren't aimed at her but at someone or something else. She paused until she was sure he was asleep again before crawling across the floor, picking up one item of clothing at a time, and carrying them in her one free hand and open mouth.

Then, remembering what she was about, Veronica silently slipped on her things. With shoes in hand she searched for Nik's building keys. Something about this old chapel compelled her to explore it.

As soon as she was outside his door, Veronica heard what she thought to be a clanging noise coming from deep within the building—not from upstairs where she'd been. She scouted around the old structure until she found a skinny door leading into what appeared to be a basement.

She tested each key until she finally found the one that unlocked the door. The door was stuck and so she used the strength of her entire body to set it free. When she finally did, she nearly fell into the dark dankness of the water-soaked room from where she thought the noise had originated. The building had suddenly turned dead quiet.

"Hello?" she whispered. "Is anyone here?"

Nothing.

Veronica was about to move further into the darkness when she suddenly heard a low growl followed by what felt like something hanging onto the back of her dress by its teeth.

***

Alfredo tossed and turned in his bed for what seemed like hours. Finally, he glanced over at his clock, three-thirty AM. He knew he should try closing his eyes one more time before rising, but he figured if he hadn't

fallen to sleep by now, he probably wasn't going to.

He rubbed his hand over his face and forced himself to get out of his

torturous bed. Why was he so restless? Why else? He was worried about

Millicent. And now both his body and brain refused to wait until later to

call her.

Normally Alfredo would never call one of his clients in the middle of

the night, but this situation was different. Millicent was different. Not only

because she was in a particularly dangerous business, but because she was

unique among his clientele.

He liked her, probably more than he should as her psychiatrist. But

who else worried about her the same way he did? Mr. Smythe? Aunt Kate?

Alfredo wasn't sure, but what he was certain of was his need to make sure

Millicent had made it home and was locked in the safety of her hotel suite.

He picked up his phone and dialed. He let it ring for what seemed like

an eternity until he finally hung up. Where was she? Why didn't she or Aunt

Kate pick up the phone? Maybe he accidently called the wrong number.

He tried again. And this time he let it ring until the hotel switchboard

intercepted.

"*Pronto*," said the voice.

"This is Alfredo Martolini. Pardon me for calling so late, but I've been

trying for several minutes to reach one of your guests and haven't been

133

able to contact her nor her aunt. I'm Millicent Winthrop's psychiatrist, and I've good reason to be concerned about her health and safety. Do you know if either she or her aunt is in?"

"I'll ring the room for you," the voice responded.

A moment passed and the voice returned. "No one's answering. I did check to see if the person you inquired about picked up her key from the concierge desk. And according to our records Signorina Winthrop returned to her suite earlier this evening."

"*Grazie.* Thank you for your time." Alfredo hung up. He thought he would somehow feel better having spoken to the switchboard operator, but no dice. In fact, his worry now bordered on panic.

That's it!

Determined to make sure Millicent was out of harm's way, Alfredo dressed quickly and ran all the way through the dawn-lit streets of Venice to the Hotel al Ponte Antico.

By the time he arrived, Alfredo was a bedraggled mess. His t-shirt hung out of his sweatpants, and it was obvious he'd forgotten to comb his hair. He hadn't even bothered to tie his tennis shoes before leaving home. The lobby was empty, so he had no choice but to ring the bell stationed on the concierge desk as he struggled to catch his breath.

An overweight, middle-aged man in a wine colored velour bathrobe appeared. "*Basta! Basta!* What's all of this noise about, signore?" It was apparent from his deep foggy voice and his unkempt manner that he, too, had just crawled out of bed.

"I need you to go to the room of Millicent Winthrop and make sure she's in. She doesn't answer my call or that of your switchboard. I'm her doctor, and I've strong reason to be worried."

The man suddenly sobered. "*Sì, sì.* Of course, signore. Let me get the pass key."

With the key in hand the gentleman in charge wheezed his way up the stairs with Alfredo following close behind. When they arrived on the floor of her suite, Alfredo scooted his way around the gradually slowing manager and began pounding on Millicent's door.

"Millicent. Aunt Kate. Open the door. This is Dr. Martolini. I need to know you're safe."

Holmes and Watson charged the door from the inside, barking at the top of their little lungs.

"Please let me try, sir," the disheveled man politely implored while the men traded places. "Signorina Winthrop, this is Signor Zamboni. Dr. Martolini and I are going to open your door on the count of three. *Mille grazie*—a thousand pardons."

With the exception of the incessant yipping from Holmes and Watson, not a sound came from the other side of the door.

"Uno, due, tre." Signor Zamboni turned the key in the lock and the door swung wide open. Out raced Holmes followed by Watson down the stairs and presumably out the front door since Alfredo didn't remember closing it when he arrived. But Alfredo wasn't concerned about their escape—only about his patient, dear Millicent.

"Millicent, are you all right? Where are you? Aunt Kate?" Alfredo and Signor Zamboni searched throughout the two bedroom suite, but no one was to be seen. What Alfredo did notice, however, caught his eye and hitched his breath. Millicent's hat and glasses sat on an end table near her bed.

Surely she wouldn't have left the suite without donning these two items.

Realizing neither woman was where they should be, Alfredo did a thorough search of the suite.

"They aren't here, Dr. Martolini. Maybe they didn't answer the phone because they're out for the evening," Signor Zamboni stated, trying to make sense of the moment.

"It's four o'clock in the morning. Where could they possibly be at four o'clock in the morning?"

Alfredo panicked.

The manager sat himself on the short blue brocade settee. "Perhaps Signorina Winthrop hasn't yet returned from her day in Nürnberg?"

Alfredo sighed in frustration. "But her hat and her glasses are here. And her suitcase is still packed and sitting on her bed. Besides, she would never knowingly leave Holmes and Watson alone for the night."

Alfredo wiped the perspiration off his face with a starched handkerchief from the pocket of this running jacket. "What worries me is her aunt's missing as well."

Signor Zamboni nodded his head. "Sì, sì."

"Look, call the police while I fetch Holmes and Watson. I'll be back with the dogs as soon as I can."

Alfredo ran down the stairs calling out for Holmes and Watson. He ran outside the hotel, but the two pugs had totally disappeared. He searched up and down the narrow streets, whistling and promising treats with each step he took.

Nearly an hour must've passed before Alfredo finally gave up and went back toward the hotel, hoping the two rascals had given up their antics and returned as well. By now the police must've arrived, he hoped. Upset and exhausted, Alfredo made his way back to the Hotel al Ponte Antico for what he hoped would be a better scenario than the one he had earlier witnessed.

***

"Good gravy, old boy. Can't you move faster than that?" Holmes was a bit testy from having been pent up in the hotel room all evening.

"'oo died and made you boss?" Watson wasn't in much better of a mood either. "I'm running as fast as my five-inch legs will carry me.

Besides, I don't know where we're running to."

"Honestly, can't you remember anything from earlier today? The scent. In the locker room at the football stadium. I am sure it is the same as what we smelled at the chapel this morning." Holmes was at a full gallop now.

"Yeah, the chapel this morning. Oh, and later at Dr. Martolini's. You're right. I, too, am sure it was the same." By now Watson had kicked it into full gear and was charging along the narrow Venetian streets alongside his mentor.

As they were about to make their turn, out jumped one of the meanest, fattest cats either pug had ever seen in their short lives. He must've weighed forty pounds or more. About the same size as Holmes and Watson put together. Watson thought him to be the spitting image of an aging Jake LaMotta of *Raging Bull* fame.

Upon seeing the cat, both pugs slid to a screeching halt. The beast sat back on his haunches and raised his paws—claws fully extended. Then the stare down began.

Holmes spoke first. "Well, well, well. If it isn't our good friend Morazzio, the rat-killer."

"Yeah, the rat-killer," Watson echoed.

"*Buona sera*, gentlemen. Or should I say, *buongiorno*." Morazzio pulled his claws in briefly to rub his face with the back of his paws. "I'm surprised to see you up so early. Had you planned some sort of surprise

attack on me and my boys? Is that why you're here at this ungodly hour?

You know, *I* run this district—this *sestieri*. Not *you* or any other of your

canine variety."

The fading moonlight glanced off of Morazzio's re-extended claws—

Boing!

—making them appear even more deadly than they did moments

ago. Within seconds, as many as thirty or more cats crept out of their

hiding spots and moved in toward the two intruders.

Holmes, ever the diplomat, decided to tread carefully with this rodent-

eating sociopath if he was ever going to reach the chapel before daybreak.

"Now, Morazzio. You know Watson and I would never think of

imposing on your territory if it weren't for a good reason. We mean you no

harm, but we do have some fear regarding the occupant of a certain chapel

in your area. I'm sure you know which one I mean."

The cat grinned through squinted eyes. "Ah, sì, I'm aware of whom

you speak. But what has this idiot to do with you, pray tell?"

This guy's a tough customer, Watson thought to himself.

Holmes continued. "Well, as you may know, we assist our mistress

Millicent Winthrop, who at this very moment is working on the case

regarding a missing mid-fielder, one Riccardo Stillitano. Now, Watson and

I have reason to believe he is being held against his will in the building by the evil man who had set up shop there."

Morazzio suddenly retracted his claws and paced back and forth in front of the two canine detectives. "Stillitano, you say? Why he's one of my favorite footballers. Kidnapped, you say? Well, why didn't you mention that in the first place? By all means, pass with care but be mindful. My spies tell me the intruder's a dangerous man doing dangerous things. And I doubt he likes dogs any more than he does cats."

All the cats meowed in agreement. And as suddenly as Morazzio and his minions had appeared, they vanished from plain sight.

"Thanks for all your help, Watson. If it weren't for my powers of persuasion, you would be nothing more than Morazzio's catnip."

"Yeah, catnip." Watson had to admit he wasn't nearly as quick on his intellectual toes as Holmes. "Sorry, 'olmes, but the rat-killer scares me nearly as much as that wicked man we're trying to track down. Maybe more, if the truth be known. But you were the dog's bullocks, if I do say so meself." Watson knew the only way to get around Holmes's bad temper was to butter him up.

Holmes cleared his throat. "Well, just so we are clear. Now let's high tail it to the chapel before we run into any more problems. Ready?"

"*Avanti*, let's go," Watson called out as he took off toward their destination with Holmes fast at his heels.

By the time the two got to the chapel the night sky had taken on the purplish pink of dawn. Only a few more minutes and the sun would crest

the Adriatic, turning the city into the golden ornament it has been for

centuries.

The two pugs circled the chapel, noses to the ground. "Do you smell

what I smell?" Holmes asked his companion.

"It's 'im, 'olmes. It's the same man from Dr. Martolini's this morning,"

announced Watson. "And the same scent as that which we uncovered at

the scene of the crime in Nürnberg. I'm sure of it."

Suddenly a noise caught their attention—a clanging noise—like

someone banging metal on metal.

"'olmes, do you 'ear what I 'ear?" Watson suddenly froze in his tracks.

"Shhh, quiet. I think it's coming from down there." Holmes nodded

his head toward a narrow basement window. "Come on, follow me. It's

time we solve this caper."

Watson started to back away. "You're not getting me to go down there.

I'd rather face Morazzio and 'is pals than deal with a pack of rats."

Holmes flapped his jowls and shook his head. "Enough now. We have

nothing to be afraid of. Besides, I am sure Morazzio has cleared this place

out of whatever vermin he and his gang could find. Now, let's get moving.

We don't have much more time left before Dr. Martolini catches up to us."

"Yeah, catches up to us. But you go first." Watson was no fool.

Holmes and Watson crept along the perimeter of the building. And were about to reach its rear quarters, when they saw a strange looking woman unlocking a door and making her way inside. Ever the alpha male, Holmes quickly assessed the situation and galloped toward the woman, growling all the way. Likewise his side kick followed only inches behind.

"Quick, Watson. We have to stop her before she is caught by that maniac." Holmes barked out orders as if he were a Marine Corp sergeant.

"But 'ow? What should I do, 'olmes?"

"The chomp, old boy. The chomp."

Immediately Watson leapt up into the air, mouth agape, and glommed onto the back of the woman's dress with his teeth. Surprised by the sudden turn of events, the woman jumped up and whacked her head on the low wooden transom above the door. She then spun around in circles, the dog attached, holding her head in pain.

"*Arrêter*, stop your growling, *s'il vous plait. Être calme. Fermer votre bouche*," she spit out with each rotation. But, it did no good at all.

Apparently the attached beast was a bit behind in his French studies, or maybe he snarled so loudly he couldn't hear her. Either way, the woman spent no time at all gathering her senses. Then faster than either Holmes or Watson thought possible, the terrified woman turned and ran down one of the shadowy walkways, away from the two ferocious animals.

"I say, Watson. Good show. That was a bloody good chomp, if I do say myself," Holmes declared proudly.

"Yeah, bloody good chomp. Now, can we get out of 'ere? This place's giving me the collywobbles!" Watson's tail went down.

"Not quite yet, old boy. We have a duty to investigate this building and locate the noise we heard earlier."

Watson plopped himself down on the pavement. "Do we 'ave to?"

"If we don't have anything more than an intruder to report to Millicent, she is not going to be pleased. And we don't want to displease our dear mistress, do we?"

Watson got to his feet. "I suppose you're right. But you go first. That way if we run into any rats, I'll be the first one out the door." And so the two pugs entered the chapel through the back basement door, wary but eager to discover whatever lay ahead.

Chapter 11

"*Pardoz-moi,* Mademoiselle Millicent. *C'est moi,* Monsieur H—pronounced ahsh." No matter how hard he tried, the Inspector couldn't seem to break into Millicent's subconscious mind. Finally, he'd no other choice but to sit on the edge of her bed and give her a bit of a shake.

"Huh?" she murmured.

"So sorry to invade your dreams so early in the morning, but I must hear about yesterday's adventure in Nürnberg. What discoveries did you make? Have you returned to Venice with any new clues?"

Millicent heard a voice faintly calling to her above the familiar strains of a dance tune played deliciously by a four-piece tango band, complete with *bandoneon*, the Argentinean equivalent to the European concertina accordion.

144

"Wha . . . ?"

Millicent was lowered into a dip by an amazingly adept male dancer, and then brought back up onto her feet again to continue the dance. As she awakened, she became aware of his left cheek pressing into her right, and of her left arm extended and held in front of her by the man's right. Something about this dance felt awkward, however.

Perhaps it was because in order to accomplish this elaborate dance with her much shorter partner, Millicent had to bend both forward and sideways at the same time.

"Ouch! Bloody hell! You stepped on my foot!" Millicent immediately broke away from the arms of her dance partner.

"Oh, so I did. *Pardonez moi encore,* Millicent. It has been some time since I've danced the tango. As a matter of fact, I'm not sure if I indeed have before this most opportune moment."

Millicent stared at the inspector in astonishment.

"Monsieur H! What are you doing here?"

Once again the detective took Millicent into his capable arms. "Why, tangoing with you, *ma chérie.*"

Locked in what felt like a vice grip, Millicent had no choice but to allow the gentleman to parade her across the dance floor before abruptly turning one hundred and eighty degrees toward the direction from which they had come.

"Well, yes, I can see that. What I mean to ask is, *to what do I owe the pleasure of this dance?*"

"Ah, *oui. C'est une bonne question.*" Once again Monsieur H leaned Millicent against his arm and swung her into a low dip before placing her back up to her feet. This time, though, he nearly dropped her, beads of perspiration surfacing on his forehead.

"Please forgive me, mademoiselle. Perhaps I'm too old for such vigorous activity, but I did want to make sure you had a bit of fun after working so diligently during these last twenty-four hours on the Nürnberg case."

Inspector H led her to a small table where two short glasses of bourbon whiskey, no ice, awaited them. Millicent gulped half her drink before coming up for air. The inspector sat patiently, lighting up one of his signature Galois cigarettes. At last Millicent spoke. "Where are we?"

"Buenos Aires, but that's beside the point," the detective said between the short intakes of his cigarette. "I wanted to confer with you about your findings at the scene of the crime. This case has me *très, très curieux.*"

"Oh, well . . . all right, I guess. Uh, I did go to the football stadium, and I did speak with the German police. Oh, by the way, you were correct. They hadn't as yet luminolled the locker room but promised me they would get right on it. I say, I'm certainly glad Mr. Smythe had met me there, the German police were somewhat hesitant in accepting me as a professional, as you might guess."

Monsieur H chuckled. "Don't bother your little head about that. I was never taken seriously either until I started solving the most impossible of cases. Then and only then was I respected. Trust me, they will clamber to accept your expertise soon enough."

"I suppose." Millicent was still confused as to why she was conversing with the inspector in an Argentinean tango parlor, while at the same time managing all the many complicated steps of a dance she'd never before this moment ever attempted.

How very odd.

"*Alors*, I was so hoping you would be able to discover something more that would help us with this investigation," he sighed and put out his cigarette.

Suddenly Millicent remembered what it was she wanted to share with this odd little man. "Actually, I made two discoveries out of my visit in Nürnberg. First of all, the villain didn't act alone. And second, if my hunch is correct, our victim's still alive."

"*C'est Fantastique.* Now all we have to do is try to follow the criminal's trail and rescue our poor footballer before the villain has a chance to change his mind and kill him." In his excitement the inspector took Millicent by the elbow and scurried out into the middle of the dance floor where the two tangoed once again. Millicent felt her heart pound. Bang,

bang, BANG!

"Millicent! Are you there, Millicent?"

Down again she went into a low dip—

Bang, *bang,* BANG!

"Millicent Winthrop, open up in the name of the law."

—and landed in her bed.

Bang, *bang,* BANG! Bang, *bang,* BANG!

"Millicent, *il mio amore.*"

"What in the bloody hell?" Millicent opened her eyes to the pounding of her door. She then listened to the voices outside her suite calling out her name. The last voice she recognized immediately as belonging to the superbly handsome Alfredo Martolini.

***

"Watson, stay close and follow me. I think I have picked up another scent which I believe I also recognize from earlier this afternoon." Holmes trotted forward into the darkness.

"Yeah, recognize." Watson also sniffed his way along the moist cement floor.

The two mini-detectives surveyed each room of the chapel basement as best they could given the lack of light. In fact, Holmes was nearly ready to give up and turn back when he once again heard the clanging noise. "Step lively, Watson. I believe that sound is coming from the room ahead."

Holmes and Watson barreled down the narrow hall and into a room partially lit from the rising sun seeping through a slender window at the top of the wall. Holmes barked to announce his arrival and Watson followed suit.

"Ahhhh . . . !" Both dogs suddenly grew quiet and held as still as they could. It was a moan all right. And it was coming from the wall adjacent to the doorway.

"Ahhhh . . . !" There it was again.

"Can you see anything, Watson?" Holmes whispered. He knew his eyes weren't as sharp as those of his friend.

Watson squinted into the darkened room. "I think so. Follow me."

This time Watson took the lead as the two pugs tip-toed into a tremendously eerie place. The smell of the musty air from the nearby lagoon as well as from the moldy walls of the abandoned chapel overtook the room. But Watson, who also had a particularly acute sniffer, foraged his way into the cave-like darkness until he at last discerned what his canine abilities had earlier guessed.

He howled once and barked twice.

"What is it, old boy?" Holmes asked, his eyes and nose not quite as yet having adjusted to the premises. Watson was already way ahead of him, jumping up and down in front of what looked to be a withered corpse.

"Ahhhh, *il mio carlino*. My little pug. Have you come to rescue me?"

149

The two sleuths recognized the man to be the missing football player kidnapped days ago from the FC Nürnberg locker room. And he was still alive. **But** barely.

When Holmes neared the man, he couldn't help but notice the footballer's bloodied face and hands.

"Come on, 'olmes. Let's get 'im out of 'ere and fast. I 'ave a feeling that 'e doesn't 'ave much longer to live if we don't."

Watson jumped onto the man's body and began licking his face.

"Wait a minute, Watson. I believe he's pinioned to the wall. Can you not see he is chained up?" Holmes, in spite of his age, was always able to assess a situation far quicker than his frisky partner.

"Yeah, chained up. So, what are we going to do?" Watson hopped up and down, nearly beside himself.

Holmes paced back and forth before stopping in his tracks. "The only thing we can do at this point. We must go back to the hotel and tell Millicent at once what we have discovered. She will know what is best. Then we can get this poor man the medical help he obviously needs."

Watson agreed. And so the two canine detectives galloped at full speed toward the Hotel al Ponte Antico as the sun finally made its full appearance in the early morning sky.

***

When Nik awoke, he felt as if he'd been hit in the head with a ten pound tube of Genoa salami. Behind the tiny slits he called eyes his vision blurred. It took him a few seconds to actually remember where he was.

As he lay in his bed it finally dawned on him that the beautiful woman whom he'd brought home was no longer with him. He smiled. It'd been a long time since someone as enchanting as the beautiful Veronica had paid much if any attention to him. He was a scoundrel, and he knew it. Nik had wanted to ravish her last night, but an evening of heavy food and alcohol left him useless.

Next time wouldn't go the same.

My God, I'm already thinking about a next time, and I've no idea where she lives, if she's married, or if she's even in the least bit interested in me.

"That was some woman, Nik," he said out loud. "Maybe the one you've searched for so long, and *idiote,* you let her get away. *Glupo, glupo, glupo*! Stupid, stupid, stupid!"

Over the years Nik had gotten used to talking to himself. Often it was the only way to deal with his constant feelings of rage and isolation.

He slowly rolled out of bed and made his way to the kitchen chair nearest the door. There he sat, head in hands, until he could get his equilibrium.

"I like that doctor," he continued. "He's a good man. Perhaps I can solicit his help in finding the beautiful Veronica. We're friends now. And what are friends for if not to help each other when the occasion arises?"

The longer he sat, the deeper Nik's thoughts went to the visitor in his basement. No matter how much he had to drink the night before, he hadn't forgotten what was at the top of his agenda. The torture and slow death of his latest victim.

Nothing—no woman, friend or sexual encounter was more important than having his revenge.

Nik stood to get a glass of water from the sink. When he did, he noticed the room spinning once again. His apartment hadn't turned so speedily, however, that he didn't notice his keys were missing from where they were supposed to be. He knew he must've brought them home with him, or how else would he have gotten inside his apartment?

But Nik wasn't at all positive that he'd placed the keys in their appropriate place before passing out onto his bed. Moving carefully but with some concern, Nik thoroughly searched his apartment. The longer he searched, the more his heart pounded within his chest. Finally a full panic set in.

Intuitively he grabbed his Makarov pistol, ran out the door and down the wooden staircase, all the time wondering if the beautiful Veronica may've been so much more than he'd originally believed. After all, it wasn't the first time he'd been duped by a beautiful woman and probably not the last.

Nik was more aware than ever of the danger his plans were falling into. If he was caught with the kidnapped football player in his basement, he would at best have to start all over again with another victim. Or at worse he would be sent to prison, and that he vowed would never happen. He would rather die first.

By the time he got to the open basement door, his gun was cocked and ready for whomever or whatever was awaiting him, be it Veronica, or a burglar, or a band of curious mongrel cats. They were all dead meat in his book.

It was unusually quiet as Nik made his way through the maze of halls and adjoining rooms. He couldn't hear a single rat, let alone the breathing of his captured prey. Carefully he entered each room, making sure no one was hiding, ready to attack. As he neared the room where he'd left the half conscious football player, he heard singing.

"Nella vecchia fattoria, ia-ia-o

Quante bestie ha zio Tobia, ia-ia-o.

C'e cane (bau!) cane (bau!) ca-ca-cane, cane (bau!)..."

Nik recognized the children's song from his youth.

"On the old farm, ee, ah, ee, ah, o!

What a lot of animals Uncle Tobias has, ee, ah, ee, ah, o!

There's a dog, bow! Dog, bow! D-d-dog..."

What the hell, thought Nik. *He's finally gone insane.*

Carefully Nik peered into the room. Nothing seemed any different

153

from when he had "visited" yesterday. Stillitano still lay on the floor with his wrists shackled. But this time instead of weeping, the man giggled like a young boy and sang a short snippet of the popular Italian nursery rhyme over and over.

"Hey, you. Be quiet." Nik made his presence known. He scanned the room once again but still didn't find anything out of place. "Who has been here? Tell me, or I will shoot you one knee at a time, and you will never play football or any other sport again."

"Bow! Bow, wow!" Stillitano sang out, obviously out of his mind.

"Tell me, dammit. Was it a woman you saw? A man?" Nik became more and more frustrated with every strain of the Italian footballer's aria.

Stillitano then whispered conspiratorially. "No woman, nor any man. It was but Hadrian, the dog of Pompeii." And then he went back to singing.

What the hell? thought Nik. He could make neither heads nor tails out of the fettered man. So he slowly backed his way out of the room, leaving the lunatic alone in his madness. He'd have to bring in a locksmith as soon as possible to secure the building. It was risky enough hiding his prisoner in the old chapel when locked, let alone when it was open and available to whomever should enter willy-nilly. He would have to move the footballer first though. But where?

***

The door to Millicent's suite flew open, revealing a sleepy bespectacled woman in a light blue flannel nightgown with matching robe sitting on the edge of the bed. Alfredo had recently wondered exactly what Millicent looked like upon awakening, but he hadn't counted on the image he now saw directly in front of him.

Buon dio, he thought. *I can't believe she actually sleeps in that silly hat, too.*

"Millicent, where've you been? You've had us worried sick." Alfredo was too tired and too shaken up to mince words. As he spoke, Holmes and Watson trotted into the suite as if nightly escapades were their normal *modus operandi.* "And you two, I've been scouring the canals and walkways of Venice looking for you all night. Why'd you run off like that? Where'd you go?"

Holmes and Watson merely sat in front of Alfredo, as if by staring up at him with their sweet googly eyes they would earn one of his delicious macaroons, or at the very least a warm pat on the head. But the doctor was far too upset over Millicent's midnight disappearance to continue rankling with the dogs.

"Yeeeaaaahhh!" Millicent let out a big yawn. "Well, let's see. I returned here from Nürnberg about eight o'clock, and then I was hungry, so I went out for a bite to eat. After that, I'm not actually sure. But I must've come home late and gone to bed, for here I am. And I could easily sleep for another four or five hours. Yeeeaaaaahhh!"

She yawned again, closing her eyes and letting her mouth drop open as she lay back onto the bed. Next thing Alfredo heard was the soft purr of snoring.

God, she has a sexy mouth. Even when she snores.

The police moved through the suite, checking closets, windows, and bathroom for unwanted guests or possible clues. Nothing seemed out of the ordinary. In fact, now that the missing woman was home safe and sound, their services were no longer needed.

"Doctor Martolini," the porculent Venetian policeman in charge said. "It appears your missing person has indeed been found."

Millicent suddenly let out a loud snort. *Snort.*

"So if you no longer need us, I think we should leave."

Alfredo sat next to the sleeping Millicent, worn out from all the activities of the frenzied night.

"*Sì, sì. Molto grazie.* Thank you for your help. I believe we're all accounted for now. Aren't we boys?" Alfredo peered down at the attentive Holmes and Watson, whose tails were wagging in adoration and the continued hope of doggie treats.

The police sergeant shook Alfredo's hand and left with his other two constables. "Anytime, Dr. Martolini. You know, it's not safe for a woman to be out so late by herself. Please, if you would speak to her about that when she awakens?"

"Don't worry. I will," Alfredo avowed.

The door shut leaving Alfredo alone on the bed next to his sleeping beauty.

"So, Signorina Millicent. Where were you tonight? And why weren't you here when I checked up on you an hour ago?"

Another snort was all that emanated from the comatose woman snoring next to him.

"And where's Aunt Kate? *O mio Dio,* you women drive me crazy, which isn't an easy thing to do. To push a skilled psychiatrist such as myself over the edge."

He took one of Millicent's hands in his own. "You drive me mad no matter what you do. I constantly worry about you, especially each time you take on a new case. I wish I'd never written that paper. Then FIFA would never have involved you in the solving of these horrible acts of violence."

Now it was Alfredo who let out a loud yawn. "*Mamma mia,* what am I going to do about you, dear sweet Millicent?" Alfredo had many more questions to ask, but they'd have to wait until later, when they were both refreshed and more able to talk. Holmes and Watson also waited for Millicent. They had many things to tell her as well, not the least of which was their discovery of the criminal and where the unfortunate Riccardo Stillitano was being held.

Yet for now, the activities of the night made it not only difficult for

Millicent to stay conscious, but for her two canine assistants as well. Even though they'd been told not to do so hundreds of times, Holmes and Watson jumped up onto Millicent's bed and snuggled in. Holmes against Millicent's body and Watson against that of Alfredo, who now also leaned back on the bed hand in hand with his vociferous client.

"*Buona notte, amica mia.* Sweet dreams my sweet," he mumbled before kissing her on the cheek.

Within seconds the only sound heard was the wheezing, snoring, and snorting of four worn out bedmates crowded together on an extremely well utilized bed.

Chapter 12

"Mmmmm," Millicent hummed. She was drowsily aware she was in the beginning stages of awakening from her late morning nap. She wanted to open her eyes, but she was far too comfortable to move. Her left leg and arm were both flung over some kind of nice warm soft pillow, and her face was buried in something fuzzy which smelt absolutely scandalous. Whatever it was, it tickled her nose.

"Tee-hee-hee!"

Alfredo woke to the sensation of Millicent stirring in his arms. She felt wonderful, and so he brought her body closer into his embrace.

"Mmmmm." There was that sound again. And then something which sounded like . . . what? A laugh?

"Shh, shh, shh," shushed the doctor. "Be quiet, my little one. *Tutto bene,* everything's fine. You're safe with me, my darling."

Alfredo proceeded to place sweet kisses all over Millicent's sleeping face—her forehead, her nose, her closed eyelids one at a time. Which wasn't the easiest of things to do given she was still wearing both that infernal hat and those ridiculous eyeglasses.

By the time he got to her mouth, unbelievably Millicent was reciprocating. Fully. "Mmmm," she moaned in appreciation.

Alfredo's eyes flew open only to see Millicent's were still tightly shut.

O mio dio, I'm not dreaming after all.

For a moment the good doctor hesitated, not sure if he was taking far too much advantage of the half-asleep Signorina Winthrop. But her response was so passionate and so extraordinarily tender, he forgot everything he knew about propriety and professional ethics and kissed her in return. The two lovers were for the first time lost in each other's kiss.

"Arf! Arf!"

Oh, bugger. Here I am in the middle of this glorious dream, kissing some handsome Italian prince and someone's dog—I shall not say who's— has to go potty.

"Arf! Arf!"

There it was again. And again.

Ciò che nel nome della santissima vergine Maria sta succedendo adesso? What in the name of the blessed Virgin Mary is going on now?

Alfredo remained lip-locked with his more than agreeable bed partner.

"*Merda.*" The word finally escaped Alfredo.

***

Millicent with lips puckered suddenly opened her eyes with a start.

"Aaaaah," she screamed at the top of her lungs, forcing Holmes and Watson to go into an even greater barking frenzy. "What the bloody hell are you doing here, Doctor Martolini?"

Both Alfredo and Millicent jumped to their feet at the same time. Millicent's glasses flew off her nose, and when she bent down to pick them up, she bonked heads with Alfredo who was attempting to do the same.

"Ouch!"

"*Mamma mia!*"

Quickly Millicent refastened her spectacles to her nose and ears. While rubbing her tender forehead she glanced up into Alfredo's big brown sleepy eyes. "I don't mean to be rude, Doctor Martolini, but were you kissing me just now?"

Alfredo rubbed what was proving to be a fairly sizeable knot on his own forehead. "Sì, Millicent. You seemed to be having a nightmare, so I was merely attempting to calm you down."

Millicent couldn't help but stare at the gorgeous hunk of Italian machismo standing before her.

Calm me down? By kissing me? Yikes.

Her mind raced while her mouth stood agape. Oddly enough, Alfredo looked rather cute in his boyish, disheveled way. Hair falling forward, clothes wrinkled, and what was that protruding behind the front of his pants?

Millicent all of a sudden hiccupped.

Oh, dear God.

Then she attempted to gather herself. "I'll have you know, *hiccup*, that a nightmare is very far, *hiccup*, from what I was experiencing. You were making a, *hiccup*, move on me, Doctor Martolini. Now, unless I'm mistaken, kissing is, *hiccup*, hardly a therapeutic tool for amnesiacs such as me."

Millicent had him there.

"No, no, signorina. You're correct. Kissing is . . . kissing is uhm . . . well, kissing is kissing. Sì, that's exactly what it is. Kissing is kissing."

The two of them stared at each other for what felt like an eternity, especially to Holmes and Watson who were nearly beside themselves with having to pee. Millicent took in a deep breath and while straightening her nightgown, she finally spoke. "It's only my opinion, but I believe we've much to discuss, Doctor Martolini."

She sped over to the chair to put on her bathrobe, straighten her hat, and wipe clean her glasses. "But first I must take the boys out for their constitutional. When I return, I presume you will still be here?"

Millicent was doing her darnedest not to make eye contact with the sexy psychiatrist standing but two feet from her bed.

Alfredo also took in a deep breath. "Why, of course, Millicent. Like you I believe it's time for the two of us to come to some kind of understanding as it were. You must know my feelings for you are much deeper than, uh, than either one of us have realized. This makes being your psychiatrist a bit tricky. But we will talk when you return, my darling."

Millicent didn't know whether to kick him in the shins or run into his arms. But there truly was no time for either action, so she quickly leashed up the two pugs, and out the door the three of them flew.

As she made her way down the winding stairs toward the open door, Millicent felt her heart beat within her chest and not because she was afraid. No, for the first time in her life Millicent felt alive with the promise of love. She giggled again merely because she couldn't stop herself.

"Tee-hee-hee."

***

"I positively do not see what's so funny, dear girl. Watson and I are about ready to explode."

"Yeah, explode."

Both of Millicent's assistants found the closest flower pot situated on the *Calle dell' Ovo* and did their business post haste.

"Please forgive my dereliction, boys. I'm actually not quite sure what's come over me, but this morning I seem to be even more forgetful than usual. And then waking up this afternoon with Doctor Martolini in my bed, well, that was, I say, that was the final straw."

Millicent stared up into the blue Venetian sky as she stood holding the leash, trying to piece together the events of the past twenty four hours. She remembered returning home from Nürnberg, but not much else until she heard Alfredo pounding on her door earlier that morning.

The only other thing she thought she remembered was dreaming of Inspector H, but none of the details of his late night visit surfaced in her mind. Yet Millicent had the feeling something else had gone on, but what she couldn't put her finger on.

Oh, bugger all. What's going on with me now?

Suddenly Millicent was pulled out of her reverie by a strong tug from Holmes's and Watson's leash.

"Millicent, yoo-hoo. I say, dear Millicent." Holmes grew more and more impatient with Millicent's frequent lapses into fantasy.

"Uhh . . . ?"

"Yeah, yoo-'oo Millicent," Watson barked even louder than usual to catch her attention.

"Oh, yes. Sorry. Having a bit of a focusing issue today." Millicent rapidly shook her head as if by doing so she'd wake up her lazy brain.

Holmes cleared his throat. "Millicent, dear. Watson and I have reason to be suspicious of the goings on in a building not too far from here. A man lies shackled to a basement wall, and I wouldn't be surprised if he very well could be our missing mid-fielder."

"Yeah, missing mid-fielder," Watson echoed.

"Oh, dear. Are you sure?" Millicent suddenly felt as if she were finally coming back to life. "What I mean to say is: how do you know the man is Riccardo Stillitano? And what for heaven's sake is he doing handcuffed to a wall in Venice, hundreds of kilometers from the scene of the crime?"

Holmes and Watson silently looked at each other for a brief moment and then trotted together several feet away from Millicent, pulling slightly on the taut leash.

"You tell 'er, mate," Watson whispered.

"I'm not going to say a word. If you want to tell her, then go right on ahead. But I'm staying out of it."

Holmes was hesitant to give Millicent too much information. No matter how much the two pugs knew about the latest case, they wanted Millicent to feel as if she were the true sleuth and not them.

Watson continued to whisper to his partner. "I'm not going to be the one to dispel Millicent's belief in 'er expertise. But what are we going to do? Pretend we didn't 'ear 'er?"

"Oh, for cat's sake. Let me handle this." Holmes and Watson pranced back to where Millicent stood still staring off into space, undoubtedly thinking about how delicious yet how improper Dr. Martolini's earlier kiss had been.

Holmes cleared his throat while Watson sniffed at the ground pretending he was on the scent of some freshly made sausages or a carton of *gelato al limon*.

"I say, Millicent, dear. We need your delicate but sensitive skill of detection in surmising whether or not Watson and I are correct in our assumption that only you can determine if the young man we believe to be still in the chapel is indeed the lost mid-fielder you seek."

Well, that explanation was convoluted enough of an answer to keep Millicent from catching on too quickly, if at all.

As soon as Watson rolled his eyes, Holmes gave him a swift kick with one of his hind legs.

"Ouch. Why did you . . . oh, yeah. The lost mid-fielder you seek." Watson may've been slow but he wasn't stupid.

"Huh? Oh, well in that case, I suspect we'd better get moving before our victim's possibly transported to another location or, God forbid, uh .. . well, you know."

Holmes and Watson barked madly and jumped up onto Millicent's gown.

"Now, now. There's no time for that. Show me the way, boys."

Millicent and her two able assistants flew along the early morning canal walkways of Venice toward the chapel investigated the day before. All the way there Millicent felt her heart pound in her chest, and it wasn't from the fact she was being pulled into a fast jog by her able assistants.

No, she was scared and suddenly overwhelmed by a sense of déjà-vu, which sort of made sense since she'd indeed been at the chapel yesterday morning. Yet somehow this felt different. Millicent was about to turn the last corner, when out of nowhere appeared an army of feral cats obstructing her way.

Holmes and Watson came to an abrupt stop with Millicent nearly tripping over them in her path. Yet as soon as Millicent took one look at the ringleader of the bunch, she turned white as the sands of the Lido. And completely passed out, falling into a neat heap no more than two feet from the furry paws of one Don Capitano Morazzio. Holmes and Watson quickly came to her aide, nuzzling her with their heads and licking her face and hands.

"Well," said Morazzio. "I see I still have a way with the ladies, sì? One look at me, and they lose all sense of reality."

Holmes was on the attack. "How dare you frighten our dear Millicent in such an impolite manner. And why in the world are you pestering us again? I thought when you gave your permission this morning for Watson and me to pass, you meant pass in general, not merely in specifics."

Watson joined his friend on his haunches and readied himself for a fight.

Holmes continued. "And look what you have done. She's out cold."

Morazzio merely licked his front paws and held Holmes in a cold stare. Finally, he spoke. "No need to get your tail in a corkscrew, my friend. I simply wanted to let you know the cats and I did a recon on the chapel this morning and discovered your footballer's no longer there."

"Bloody hell! Are you sure?" Holmes asked.

"Yeah, bloody 'ell," Watson, of course, added.

Before Morazzio could go into detail or snipe back with a snide comment, their collective attention was unexpectedly transfixed on the crumpled form of Millicent, who moaned from where she lay. In fact, her whole body shook. Holmes and Watson hurried to lay down by her side, while an army of bedraggled cats circled in and stared at the odd woman laying the pavement.

Watson and Holmes stared at one another with their googly eyes and then remarked in unison, "Here we go again."

"What in the name of the Virgin Mary is happening? I didn't mean to kill her, *miei cari amici*, my dear friends. You must believe me," Morazzio cried, visibly shaken.

"Shhh, be quiet, will you? Millicent is going into one of her spells, that's all. But we must all be quiet and not move a muscle, or she may not come out of it, or at least not in one piece."

"Yeah, in one piece," Watson whispered.

Millicent lay like a load of ill-folded laundry surrounded by two dreadfully concerned pugs and at least fifty puzzled yet curious Venetian cats. They watched her intently and huddled in close to listen should she say something, but all they heard was a loud but contented snore.

***

Millicent as Millicent was out cold. Yet by taking on the viewpoint as the criminal, Millicent was alive and in action.

In her mind she was no more in a crumpled heap beside the Accademia Bridge than she was sipping tea and eating chocolate biscuits on the top of Mount Everest. No, Millicent was hard at work releasing a pair of handcuffs from the wrists of a lunatic singing what sounded like *Old MacDonald Had a Farm* at the top of his lungs—and in Italian, no less. She could feel herself breathing heavily and breaking into a sweat.

"*Umikni idiote!* Shut up, you idiot! If you don't, I'll have to kill you and forget about whatever satisfaction I was hoping to get from torturing you." Millicent heard the man's voice as it emanated from her own lips. But the crazed victim could only laugh and sing another verse of the children's nursery song at top volume.

"*E per la sua azienda aveva un pesce—ia—ia—o!*"

That did it. Millicent could feel her wheels turn as if in a panic.

"Very funny, you *idiote*. *Un pesce* . . . a fish. I'll show you a fish." She crossed the cell floor and found a rag next to a plastic bottle filled with a liquid. She unscrewed the lid, which allowed the most noxious of vapors to be released into the air. While holding her breath, Millicent poured a dab of the contents onto the rag.

"You leave me no other choice, Mister Pagliacci Football Player."

And with that she placed the cloth over the nose of the madman. As he slumped over she could hear herself say, "You and I are going to take a little boat ride together, Signor Stillitano. Yet until I can make arrangements, I'm going to have to hide you somewhere other than here. This cell's been compromised."

Millicent took one look at the midfielder and knew this was going to be no small feat. The first thing she had to do was get him out of the basement, and then up the stairs to her apartment above the north transept of the chapel. All this and with a body of dead weight as well.

Quickly she hoisted the fragile man over her shoulder. "Ooof!" She then carefully made her way out from the underground crypt and up the set of steps at the back of the building, all the while making sure no one saw her do so.

"*Majka Božja!* Mother of God! My back can't take any more stupid mistakes," Millicent complained.

Twenty minutes later she threw her unconscious victim onto the bed in front of her. Hours would pass before he would wake. This she knew. But Millicent wasn't going to take any chances. She speedily ripped the top sheet into strips of cloth. She then dragged Stillitano over to one of the chairs and with the pieces of sheet, tied him to it.

Next she covered his mouth with tape in case he cried out for help, or worse, sang yet another verse of *Old MacDonald.* When she had the young man secured, she whipped out her cell phone and called a familiar number.

"Luca, Nik. I have another job for you. Meet me at the pier—*Rio dell' Albero*—with your speedboat in five minutes."

"It's physically impossible to get there in five—" said the voice at the other end of the line.

"Five minutes or else."

Millicent heard a faint, distant calling from the recesses of her mind. "Five. I say, five" it echoed.

Funny, but she thought she recognized that voice. It certainly wasn't coming from her for a change.

"Millicent, dear. We're counting from five. If you don't snap out of this before we finish, it's the hospital for you."

Oh. She was familiar with that voice. And the clearing of the throat.

(Eh-ah-hum) "Four . . ."

"Yeah, four."

Snort. Millicent was aware of that voice as well. "Tee-hee-hee."

"Three . . . Wait! Did I hear you giggle, dear lady?"

"Yeah, three—tee-hee-hee."

"Quiet, Watson. I believe she is coming to." Holmes didn't mean to be so bossy toward his dear friend Watson, but as the alpha, it was in his DNA.

"*Ringraziare la Vergine*. Thank the Virgin," sighed Morazzio. And the entire cat mafia mewed in chorus to their leader's incantation.

Holmes and Watson saturated Millicent's face with their licking, including her glasses, in an effort to bring her out of her current stupor.

"Speak to us, Millicent."

"Yeah, speak."

"Two . . ." moaned Millicent as she felt herself beginning to float back into reality.

Millicent woke with a start, and a snort, and leapt to her feet. She searched around her, unable to focus at first due to her severely smudged glasses. Taking them off, she quickly cleaned them with the hem of her skirt.

"One," Millicent exclaimed as she returned her glasses to her nose and then giggled with delight at the information her recent trance had illuminated.

"Tee-hee-hee."

As she bent to pick up their leash, Millicent ran her hand over the thick fur of the chubby cat in front of her. Morazzio instantaneously purred in ecstasy.

"What a cute little pussy, pussy, pussycat," sang Millicent in baby talk.

"Pussy? Bah!" shrieked Morazzio, flying through the air and landing several feet away. As he and his followers scurried off into the darkened canal alleyways, Holmes and Watson could hear their new friend exclaim, "Good luck, *il mio piccolo Carlini*. Be safe. But keep that woman as far away from me as possible. Meeeeeeoooooow."

"Goodness, temperamental isn't he?" Millicent remarked. "Come, boys, we've no time to waste. Tally ho."

With leash in hand Millicent raced toward the Accademia Bridge only to be thrown flat onto her backside by two reluctant pugs holding their ground. "Oof!" Millicent exclaimed. As she gazed straight up into the hovering faces of Holmes and Watson, she gave them a piece of her befuddled mind.

"What's the bloody matter with you two? I thought we had no time to lose."

Holmes cleared his throat, *bluh-bluh*. "Dear Millicent, have you lost your bearings completely? We are to head towards the chapel. You remember the chapel, don't you?"

"Yeah, don't you?" Watson asked with a look of concernment on his goofy but all too familiar face.

Millicent searched her brain, but she couldn't remember a chapel to save her life. Her mind was a total blank.

"Oh, why yes, of course, the chapel," she lied as best she could, not wanting to alarm the boys anymore than she already had.

As Millicent stood to her feet, Holmes and Watson gave each other a knowing look of trepidation. Finally, Holmes spoke. "So sorry, dear lady. Please forgive me. Perhaps I hadn't made myself totally clear. You'd better hang on tightly to the leash for Watson and I know the way."

Pulling Millicent behind them at breakneck speed, the pugs galloped toward the chapel as fast as their little legs could carry them. All three sleuths were determined to find Riccardo Stillitano as swiftly and as stealthy as possible. After all, his life depended upon it.

Chapter 13

As he hoisted the young footballer over his shoulder, Nik felt as if he were being watched. Yet he didn't see a single soul, with the exception of a few canal cats. It took all of his strength, plus some, to carry the comatose Riccardo Stillitano up the stairs and into his apartment.

Normally Nik wouldn't have been so weak, but last night's drinking had left him dehydrated and shaky. Well, dehydrated anyway. Shaky was probably a result of his encounter with the bewitching Veronica Nero.

Nik fantasized about this enchanting woman as he tied up his hostage and secured duct tape over the crazy man's mouth. Questions as to where she lived and when he would ever see her again played like a tape recorder over and over again in his brain.

He tried to remember everything the two of them had talked about and had done in his apartment, but his memory was hazy. How long she'd stayed and what time she'd left his bed were a mystery to him. However, he was sure of one thing. As much as he desired her, they hadn't made love.

Za ljubav Allah—for the love of Allah. That I would've remembered.

At first he considered Veronica had been the one to have stolen his keys and to have unlocked the chapel's basement door, but he quickly dismissed that thought based on what he knew to be true in his heart. She'd found him desirable. More desirable than he could've imagined himself to be. And she'd come to his home and his bed without hesitancy. She'd lain in his arms until he'd at last fallen asleep. Besides, it was already past noon, and still the police weren't as yet pounding on his door.

Luca by now should be waiting for him in a nearby hidden canal. Nik had no idea as to where the two of them were going to hide the sought-after Riccardo Stillitano, but he knew Luca would more than likely have an idea. He was about to run out of his apartment door when Nik heard noises coming from the basement. Barking. But even more threatening—human footsteps.

***

Where is that woman? God in Heaven. Dio in cielo. She should've been back a long time ago.

Alfredo was a patient man, except when it came to his concerns regarding Millicent Winthrop. No question about it—Millicent embodied an acute intelligence and sophistication in the art of sleuthing, but she admittedly was a bit of a scatter-brain as well. Probably due to her issues around amnesia, but then again, maybe not. Who knew for sure? Alfredo certainly didn't have a clue, and he was a professional.

Yet the more he worked with Millicent, the more he realized the layers of her disorder were deep and not always readily visible. She was a complex woman, which was part of her challenge as well as her charm.

Not wanting to jump the gun and call in reinforcements, Alfredo decided to take a quick look outside to see if Millicent and the pugs were in sight.

And what about Aunt Kate? Where has she been all this time?

Alfredo's thoughts swirled around in his mind. He was definitely having issues piecing together the entire situation so as to make some kind of sense of it. Usually when this kind of thing happened, all the good doctor needed to do was walk through the beloved streets, piazzas, and canal-ways of Venice. Then as if by magic his thoughts would somehow coalesce into a kind of logical order.

Hoping this would be the case today, Alfredo circled back toward his home and office in the Dorsoduro by way of Saint Mark's Square. He knew how much Millicent loved the old basilica and piazza along with its Doge Palazzo and Bridge of Sighs. Besides, he wouldn't put it past her to wander off in that direction and get solidly sidetracked—pugs or no pugs.

The longer he searched, however, the more he realized Millicent, Holmes, and Watson were nowhere to be seen. Alfredo was beginning to panic, and so asked everyone he met—old and young, tourist and resident alike—if they had seen a woman matching her description. He had absolutely no luck until a little boy named Paolo said he knew who the three missing detectives were, but he hadn't seen them that particular morning.

"Are you sure you know of whom I speak?" Alfredo had to be certain of the child's memory.

"*Sì, sì.* The woman with the funny hat and glasses, who likes *gelato al limon* exactly like me. I know her and her little pugs—*il suo piccolo carlini.*"

The boy could see the man was visibly shaken. "Please, let me help look for them with you. *Per favore,* signore."

"*Bene, bene.* All right, all right. But stay close to me, in case we run into danger."

In that moment, Alfredo's cell phone rang and by looking at the caller ID "restricted," he knew the call could only be from one person.

"*Buon pomeriggio,* Mr. Smythe. I was about to call you."

***

With a sense of déjà vu Millicent immediately recognized where the three of them at last were—the chapel of Watson's unseemly inauguration the morning prior. Yet something else about the building felt familiar to her as well, even though she couldn't as of yet put her finger on it.

Moments and feelings like these always threw Millicent for a loop, causing her to doubt her own imaginal gifts and detective smarts. She was sure the information was somewhere in her brain, but how to access it was another story.

The building stood stone cold silent, defying the sun as if it were a decaying crypt filled with ghosts and whisperings. Millicent's own statue-like body mirrored the chapel's impenetrable façade. She wanted to move forward and rescue the hostage, but some internal voice telling her to stay her ground kept her frozen in place.

"This way Millicent." Holmes pulled on the leash.

"Yeah, this way—be'ind the building." Millicent felt the leash being towed by Watson as well.

"Huh?"

"Millicent, dear lady, are you not feeling up to pursuing this?" Holmes was ever vigilant as far as the workings of Millicent's mind were concerned. And lately it appeared to him she was in some ways more fragile than ever.

"Uh . . . yes, but . . . ." Millicent gawked at her feet. Her brain told her to go forward, but her gut told her to stay. Or even better, to retreat.

Holmes and Watson pranced back toward Millicent and sat directly in front of her, forcing her to look both dogs directly into their googly eyes.

"Now listen here, dear lady," Holmes began. "That young man in there needs your wit and expertise to free him from the danger he most obviously is in. And if we do not make our advance now, who knows what may become of young Riccardo Stillitano."

"Yeah, Riccardo Stillitano."

Millicent briskly shook her head back and forth as if to get all her marbles in order. As if by some magical force Millicent suddenly heard a new voice in her head, and this time it wasn't from her own fears but from some knowing place within her psyche.

They're right and you know it. Now, take a deep breath, stand up straight, and look lively because today will prove the culmination of your destiny.

If she wasn't mistaken, the voice sounded an awfully lot like that of Aunt Kate.

Or perhaps Monsieur H.

"Then lead the way boys."

With the help of Holmes and Watson Millicent found herself standing in front of an open basement door behind the chapel. In the blink of an eye she and the dogs were inside the cellar of the old building in search of the missing footballer. The boys led her to where they'd last seen Stillitano, but he was no longer there. The cell was empty and the shackles released.

"Oh hell, I can't believe our misfortunate timing." Millicent was more angry than sad, so she stamped her foot and clenched her fists in frustration.

"Millicent, look over here." Holmes drew her attention to a bottle of spirits and an odiferous rag lying next to it.

"Yeah, over 'ere."

"Aha, as I imagined," she said. "Whoever that rat is, he's using chloroform to knock out his prey before he abducts them and hides them wherever his will. Ooo, he's making me bloody furious."

Suddenly the dogs began barking. Millicent was about to scold them when she heard footsteps behind her.

"I wish to apologize for any inconvenience I may've imposed upon you, signorina. But I think this charade has finally come to its inevitable end. Yes?" Millicent turned around and looked directly at the man with the voice. As soon as she did, she let out a tiny shriek.

"Eek!"

"Eek, indeed. Wait a minute. I know you. And I recognize these two whatever-they-are, as well."

Millicent held her breath. She also found the man's face and demeanor familiar but was having her usual problems pinpointing exactly who he was and where she'd seen him before.

Damn memory.

"They're pugs—a breed associated with British royalty, and descended from the dynastic courts of the Chinese—if you must know."

Well, at least I remembered that.

The man let out a loud guffaw. "Ha, you don't say."

Holmes and Watson bared their teeth and growled.

The man stepped toward Millicent while pulling out his revolver. "I suggest you tell me what it is you're doing here besides trespassing on my property."

Millicent blew him a raspberry. "Pfff! This is no more your property than the Doge Palazzo is mine."

Her legs noticeably began to shake.

Holmes and Watson gathered around Millicent, appearing as though they were ready to lay siege at any moment upon the man, in spite of his weapon.

"Be that as it may, I'm afraid I can't allow you to leave, for there's no doubt in my mind you'll tell the good doktor it was me who has kidnapped the footballer."

"Good doctor?"

Bugger all. Why can't I piece this together?

"Come, signorina. Surely you don't take me as a fool? Alfredo Martolini, of course."

Millicent's mouth fell open.

"What is it? Don't tell me—you both work for Interpol, yes? Or is it MI6? Or Italy's ridiculous equivalent, the AISI?"

Millicent's wheels were turning. She faintly remembered the man but still couldn't place him. "I've no idea what you're speaking of, sir. My dogs ran away from me, and I hadn't caught up with them until they scampered into this building."

Now, Millicent was many things, but a good liar wasn't one of them.

The man guffawed even louder than before. "I don't know who you're trying to fool, but I think it's best that you come with me until I can figure out what it is I'm going to do with you." He pointed his gun toward the open basement door and then back at her and the pugs. "After you, signorina."

Millicent crossed her arms and held her stance. "*Oh, pour l'amour de Dieu! C'est ridicule!*"

Where the hell did that come from?

Nik stared at the woman in shock. "So . . . you must be with the French police. Is that it?"

"For heaven's sake. I'm not French, you imbecile. I'm British and *you're* an even bigger fool than I perceive you to be if you think you can get away with this." Millicent grew braver and braver as the seconds passed. Which was totally unlike her, as she noted. But the feeling didn't last long.

The red-faced man, obviously irate, charged toward her and grabbed her right arm. With the revolver pressed to her temple he proceeded to push her awkwardly through the door, while Holmes and Watson barked and jumped up onto his legs the entire time.

"You need to shut up, and that goes for your dogs, too, or I will shut them up permanently."

"You wouldn't."

Nik emitted a cynical laugh. "Oh, but I would. And I wouldn't think twice about shutting you up as well."

Millicent hiccupped.

Holmes and Watson must've understood the intent of the man with the gun, for they both immediately stopped what they were doing and sat their hindquarters on the floor.

"Millicent, dear, Watson and I are going to have to get help. We can't stop this despicable character by ourselves. But have no fear, dear lady. We will return faster than you can say 'Fédération Internationale de Football Association'."

"Yeah, what 'e said."

"All right, boys. Time to be good little pugs like I know you can be." Millicent conveyed as best she could that she understood what Holmes and Watson had said without giving away their next action. She knew she must create some kind of diversion, but what?

By Jove, I've got it!

Millicent abruptly stopped in her tracks.

"Ooooooooohhhhh!" She grabbed her head with her loose hand and swerved.

"Ooooooooohhhh!" Millicent moaned louder. Suddenly she turned and threw herself onto her opponent. As she slid down his unresponsive body, she continued to wail at the top of her lungs. "Ooooooooohhhh!"

Nik had no other recourse but to stop pointing the gun at Millicent's head and help her to the floor. In that moment, the dogs took the opportunity to make their getaway.

Dropping the semi-comatose actress to the floor—

"Eek!"

—Nik took off running after the two escapees. But they were far too fast and far too crafty for him. Holmes and Watson had one gear and one gear only, so it was full tilt boogey to the Hotel al Ponte Antico.

***

"Doctor Martolini. Alfredo," Mr. Smythe said gingerly, "I apologize for not calling you sooner, but we're currently in the process of narrowing our circle of entrapment around the criminal, the one Millicent has been helping us track down."

Alfredo couldn't believe his ears. "I was going to call you myself when my phone rang."

Mr. Smythe continued. "I've tried to get a hold of her all morning, but she isn't answering her phone, which worries me immensely. Do you happen to know where she is?"

"No, I don't know where Millicent is, or Aunt Kate for that matter.

And it's worrying me to the point of madness. Millicent left the suite about an hour ago to take Holmes and Watson out for a walk, and in her night clothes no less, but she has yet to return."

The phone went silent for a moment. Finally, Alfredo broke the silence. "Hello? Mr. Smythe?"

It was worse than Mr. Smythe had imagined. He always knew Millicent would one day be in danger's way, but he hoped that day could be avoided with his and Doctor Martolini's vigilant assistance.

"I'm right here, Alfredo. But listen carefully. It's extremely possible Millicent may be in great peril. Early this morning an informant called to let me know she'd seen the missing football player and that he's chained to a wall in the basement of an abandoned building not far from your home and office. If Millicent and the dogs are anywhere near that chapel, they could find themselves in a threatening situation. You understand?"

"Sì, of course. But what can I do?" To Mr. Smythe Alfredo sounded frantic. Realizing he had to be profoundly exact and authoritative in what he next said to Alfredo, Mr. Smythe minced his words carefully.

"Where are you now?"

"I'm with a young boy named Paolo and we're near San Marco Square."

"Stay where you are," Mr. Smythe ordered. My men and I are not far from you. Once we establish a perimeter around the chapel, which should be within the next few minutes, someone will come and get you. I want to make sure everything's safe first, so don't try any heroics. I don't want to have to worry about you as well as the boy."

The sweat rolled off of Alfredo's brow. "No, no, of course not. We will wait for you here as instructed."

"Oh, and by the way, my informant also told me Millicent's Aunt Kate was seen leaving the Hotel al Ponte Antico very late last night with several pieces of luggage. It was the guess of the informant that Aunt Kate planned a long journey. Perhaps a cruise through the Greek Islands or a river trip down the Danube."

"Yes, perhaps."

***

Alfredo didn't know whether to feel relief or abject terror. As soon as he hung up the phone, he knelt down and looked Paolo straight in the eye. "Do you have any idea where this chapel might be?"

Paolo's eyes began to light up as a subtle smile crossed his lips. "Sì, I think so, signore."

"Then what do you say we go find Millicent and the pugs before they find themselves in even more trouble." Alfredo's smile matched that of the boy.

"*Sì, signore. Avanti!*"

Hand in hand the two rescuers left the piazza and wound their way through the canal streets toward what the young Paolo believed was the building in question.

Chapter 14

"*Srati!* Shit! Stupid dogs!" Nik could hardly contain his anger as he paced the floor. How could he have allowed himself to be duped by two pint-sized canines? And ugly ones at that. The only thing he was sure of was he had to get rid of the woman on the floor in front of him, but how?

First, he had to get her out of this basement and fast. Should somebody looking for her find her here, his maniacal plan would come to an abrupt end. This day was definitely not turning out the way he'd intended.

Where did I go wrong?

Nik ran his hand over his face and thought about what he needed to do next. Not sure whether the crazy woman in front of him had truly fainted or not, Nik decided the best thing to do was make sure she couldn't give him any more trouble.

Make Mine The Italian

Quickly he went for the bottle of chloroform resting on the floor and without hesitation put the newly saturated rag up to Millicent's mouth and nose. "Eek" was all he heard as the woman who already lay folded on the floor before him unfurled herself into a completely outstretched position, not unlike a beach-stranded starfish.

"Yes. Now we're back in business," he said as he pulled her up over his shoulder. Once again he had to make the trek out of the basement and up his back stairs to the apartment where Mr. Stillitano lay awaiting his fate.

Srati. How can such a little woman weigh so damn much?

Millicent was in no position to answer, with her bottom facing the heavens and her head bobbing against the man's lower back. How she kept her hat and glasses on was nothing short of a miracle. Nik was forced to stop several times while carrying her up the stairs so as to catch his breath.

He was definitely going to need Luca's help in removing both this woman and Stillitano from his apartment to some new hideout. And with Luca's speedboat at his disposal, he could easily find a new place to hide on either the Italian or Slovenian coasts.

As soon as he entered his apartment, Nik threw the half-comatose woman down on his unmade bed. More than five minutes had passed since he'd last spoken with Luca, so he had no choice but to hurriedly tie Millicent to the remaining vacant chair and tape her mouth closed. No way was he to be waylaid by some idiot woman yelling for help.

He placed Millicent on the opposite side of the room as the football player. No use risking the two of them helping each other escape. When he finished, Nik tore down the stairs toward the canal where Luca's boat lay moored. A smug grin formed on his face as he thought to himself how much smarter he was now than he'd ever before realized. Certainly smarter than any police department or intelligence organization standing in his way.

Even the French police can't stop me and my plans to bring FIFA to ruin.

He laughed out loud despite the looks from the people strolling through the canal streets on this crisp yet sunny autumn afternoon.

***

"Ohaay! Ohaay!" Millicent lay back with her eyes closed against the cushioned prow of a gondola and listened to the gondolier's familiar call as he warned others he needed to turn a sharp left into a narrow sun-bleached canal. The sound of the water from the gondolier's oar lapped against the sides of the skiff and lulled her into a dreamy state of unconsciousness.

This was heaven. The only thing which could make this afternoon more pleasant would be if the handsome Alfredo were riding in the gondola with her, holding her in his arms.

"Psst, Mademoiselle Winthrop."

Oh, bother. Now who could that be?

"Please, Mademoiselle Millicent. You must listen to me. You're in extreme danger, but never fear. Help's on its way."

Oh, no. It can't be?

Millicent half-opened her puffy drugged eyelids and turned around in her seat. There standing on the top of the prow was none other than Inspector H in a white and navy striped shirt wearing a red scarf around his neck.

"Monsieur H! What are you doing piloting this gondola? And how in the blazes did I even get here?"

"Trivialities, mademoiselle," he said as he quickly lit his Galois cigarette. "What's important now is for you to turn your head around and close your eyes once again while I tell you what's in store for you up ahead."

Oh, for criminy sake!

Millicent hated to be told what to do, but her eyelids felt so heavy, it was difficult for her to do much else but follow this peculiar man's gentle instruction.

"*Voilà.* That's it, mademoiselle."

Millicent felt the gondola make another left turn, this time into a dark deserted alleyway. "Ohaay, ohaay." She could hear Monsieur H call as if from afar. His sonorous voice and the slap of the water against the boat drew her into a hypnotic state heavy with mist and fog.

"Whatever happens the rest of this day, simply know you're a superb detective. The young man you save today will owe his life to you and your expertise. Trust your instincts, your creativity and, most of all, your heart."

"Mmmmmm . . . ."

"You're truly a unique and talented sleuth, my dear, but you must be careful of the man who calls himself—"

As the gondola floated in and out of the canals of Venice, all that could be heard was the sound of her gentle snoring.

***

Millicent had no idea as to how long she'd been out when she awakened by the loud snort which came from none other than her. Judging from the size of her headache, however, her *nap* must've lasted a good fifteen or twenty minutes. Barely long enough for her to be transported to another room and her hands and feet tied to a wooden chair. She felt nauseous and as if she couldn't breathe.

At first she thought she was having an all-too-familiar panic attack, but then she noticed her mouth was taped shut. As she lifted her head to get more air in through her nose, she spotted a man across from her who likewise was tied to a chair with his mouth taped as well. She squinted her fuzzy-visioned eyes and recognized him immediately—Riccardo Stillitano.

"Mmmmm mmm mmm mmm," she called out to him, forgetting there was no way he could possibly understand. Even with her mouth

193

uncovered, Millicent spoke little or no Italian, English after all being her native tongue.

Stillitano sat like a statue in his own wooden chair. His head bent forward, chin on his chest. Millicent tried again—

"Mmmmm mmm mmm mmm."

—but to no avail. The man was out cold.

Fortunately the chair wasn't nailed to the floor. With all her strength and agility Millicent rocked back and forth, inching her way toward the footballer. She even tried scooting, but she couldn't seem to get anywhere fast. After all, now both of their lives depended upon her craftiness as well as her speed. She was left with no other choice but to tip the chair over with herself in it onto the floor and roll.

It was cumbersome as all get-out at first, but finally Millicent got the hang of it. Right side of legs to floor. Then chair up over her back with forehead, knees and shins to the ground. Chair flipped over to the left. And then onto the back of the chair with eyes facing the ceiling.

She had but three of those rotations in her before she knew her body would give out. Nonetheless, she went for it, which was quite a trick. For all this time she'd been able to still keep her glasses and hat firmly affixed.

Good thing my body's strong enough for all this foolishness. I suppose I owe it to all the rigorous exercise I get walking Holmes and Watson, or should I say, when they walk me.

When Millicent finally made it to Stillitano's chair, she tried nudging him with her body.

"Mmmmm, mmm, mmm, mmm." No movement whatsoever.

Oh, bollucks! Now normally Millicent wouldn't make the choice she knew she needed to make in that moment, for it could possibly result in this fine athlete becoming hurt. But she had no other recourse but to hope that by tipping Stillitano over onto his back, she might startle him out of his stupor. With each other's help, they could very well escape their bindings.

Un, deux, trois . . . huh? Bloody hell. Why am I counting in French?

As soon as Riccardo Stillitano hit the ground, his eyes flew open. "Eh?"

***

Ah, the Madonna of Mercy. La Madonna della Misericordia. She's here at last to set me free. But why is the Madonna in a nightgown and wearing a hat and those ridiculous glasses? And why is she tied to a chair?

By this time Millicent's face hovered over the handsome but battered face of the kidnapped midfielder. She batted her eyes at him. She then turned him over onto his side. After doing the same, she then maneuvered herself so that her fingers touched the ropes tied around his wrists. When they finally loosened, Stillitano reached up and removed the tape from his mouth and the bindings from his feet.

"*Ringrazio il mio bellissimo angelo.* Thank you my beautiful angel. You've come to save me at last."

"Mmmm, mmm, mmm, mmm." Millicent still was unable to converse, but Stillitano merely guessed that she wanted to at least let him know she fully accepted the compliment.

As quickly as a recently chloroform-sedated person could manage, Stillitano untied Millicent's hands and feet. And as gently as he could, he tore away the tape from her mouth.

***

"Oh, Twig and Berries." More often than not Millicent kept her expletives to herself, but damn, that smarted. Now she really did feel like throwing up.

"Riccardo Stillitano, I presume?" she asked.

"Sì, sì. I think it's still me." He gave her a wink.

Oh, those Italians.

"By the way, where am I?"

Millicent had almost forgotten the last place the young athlete had been free was in the locker room of the F.C. Nürnberg stadium.

"Oh, yes. Well, you see. You were kidnapped in Germany by a very evil person, and he has held you here at this abandoned chapel since your arrival in Venice four days ago. I've had some difficulty finding you. And honestly, for the last two days I thought you'd already been killed. But here you are—no worse for wear—I must say." She nervously giggled. "But we must leave this place as quickly as possible before the man returns to do his dirty work. Can you walk?"

"Let me try. I must admit I haven't been myself these last few days. The man of whom you speak is indeed an evil man. But I've been visited by everyone from the Virgin Mary and a beautiful angel with long dark hair, to you, whoever you are, signorina. So, in spite of my circumstance, I was blessed nonetheless." Riccardo paced the room—slowly at first and then picking up speed.

Millicent blushed. One, because of the compliment, and two, because Riccardo was one fine specimen of a fully matured man. "Uh, look, we need to get out of here post haste. I don't know why we've been left here by ourselves, but I do know that horrible man isn't going to let us stay here much longer."

"I agree, signorina. I believe I'm ready whenever you are."

"Then let's make our escape, shall we?"

Suddenly the two of them heard footsteps on the stairs, then a booming voice singing a tune, which somewhere in the back of Millicent's mind she thought she recognized from who-knows-when before.

"Oh, bugger," she whispered.

"Quick, signorina. Hide."

***

Assuming Alfredo Martolini would still be there waiting, Holmes and Watson sped as fast as they could through the canal streets of Venice toward Millicent's hotel room.

"Get the lead out, 'olmes. We 'aven't got all day." Watson loved teasing Holmes about his weight, even though Holmes was only a few pounds heavier than his littermate.

Holmes's protruding tongue nearly scraped the ground as he ran. "I'm scampering as fast as I am able, thank you very much."

Holmes panted all the way passed the hotel doors and up the stairs to the suite. The door was ajar, and both boys raced across the threshold, barking at the tops of their little lungs.

As soon as he flew into the living area, Watson threw himself down onto the rugged floor, snorting away between yips. Holmes, not seeing the doctor upon first entering, did a thorough search of the entire suite before he came to realize the apartment was indeed empty—no Alfredo Martolini. He then limped toward Watson and collapsed in front of him trying with difficulty to catch his breath.

"He's not here, old boy." Snort—snort. "We'll have to catch him at his office." Snort—snort. "That is, if he is even there." Snort—snort—snort.

Not knowing when to keep himself in check, Watson continued to poke at his friend. "You look at bit knackered, 'olmes. I bet I could race ya there and win, you ol' geezer."

Holmes immediately stood up and bared his crooked under bite. "Don't you dare be cheeky with me, you shirty Todger. I'm but a few seconds older than you, Mr. Watson. Besides, this is no time for us to be acting silly, when our own dear Millicent is in dire trouble."

Watson grinned sheepishly at his best friend. "Sorry, 'olmes. Sometimes I can't 'elp myself." He giggled softly to himself.

With that the two super sleuths scampered out the door and onto their familiar path leading to the home and office of Alfredo Martolini. They hadn't gotten any further than the Accademia Bridge, however, when Watson blurted out, "'olmes, look. Over there. Isn't that Paolo?"

"You're absolutely correct, Watson. And if I am not mistaken, I believe we've also found our dear Doctor Martolini."

Yeah, Doctor Martolini."

***

Alfredo couldn't believe his eyes. He and Paolo had been wandering the neighborhood for what seemed forever searching for the deserted chapel. Yet no sooner had he and Paolo turned the corner near the Ponte dell'Accademia, there before them trotted Millicent's beloved dogs. He whistled to draw their attention, even though they were already making their way toward him and his new little friend.

At first Alfredo was excited to see them, but then felt his heart sink. Under no circumstances whatsoever would Holmes and Watson be wandering the canal streets without their mistress unless she was incapacitated or in deep trouble.

Watson flew into Paolo's arms while Alfredo stooped down to cuddle Holmes. "My little pugs, *il mio piccolo carlini*, where's your mistress? We must find her and quickly—*rapidamenta*—no?"

As quickly as they had appeared, Holmes and Watson scurried away from the doctor and the little boy toward the chapel. Then as if to coax Alfredo and Paolo to follow, Holmes and Watson abruptly stopped, turned to face the two Italians, and barked intensely.

"No, no. Come back here my little friends. Don't run away now that we've found you." Alfredo couldn't bear to lose Millicent and her precious dogs all in the same day.

Holmes and Watson trotted back, but only to turn and scamper away again.

Paolo tugged on the jacket sleeve of the worried doctor. "I think they want us to follow them, Signor Alfredo. They must know better than you and me where Millicent was last seen."

"Sì, you're probably right, Paolo. Come. Let us follow these two, but be careful. We may not be as safe as we assume to be."

Taking the boy's hand, Alfredo chased after Holmes and Watson as they galloped toward the chapel, the place where they had last visited the sad mid-fielder.

200

Chapter 15

Bloody hell!

As soon as Millicent had gone to all the trouble of freeing herself and Riccardo Stillitano, who should appear, but that horrible man with the gun and the knock-out juice. He was truly starting to get on Millicent's nerves. Plus, she absolutely couldn't stand a man wearing a wrinkled suit.

"Signorina," Riccardo whispered, "stand behind me, and when he comes through the door, I'll take him by surprise."

Immediately the midfielder picked up one of the tipped-over chairs and held it over his head, ready to send it careening down upon the skull of his approaching perpetrator. Millicent hid herself several feet behind him.

Nik had learned many years ago to be hyper-vigilant in his every action. As he neared the door to his apartment, he took out his gun, ready to shoot whoever should come between him and his evil purpose. He carefully turned the doorknob of his unlocked door and flung it open, only to find both of his hostages missing.

What the hell? Srati, srati, Srati. I must be the most hated of all men, otherwise why would Allah punish me so?"

Not totally sure where the idiot footballer and that female menace were, Nik slinked into his room in a sideways manner. Yet as soon as he crossed the threshold, he found himself face to face with a man with a loaded chair.

"Forgive me, signore," Riccardo cried out as he lowered the chair with all his strength, which wasn't much given how weak he'd become over the last four days of his captivity. Nik dove out of the way in time to see the chair hit the floor and shatter into a hundred pieces.

Millicent screamed.

"Eek!"

Nik then raised his gun with both hands and was ready to shoot Riccardo when he unexpectedly heard the footsteps of whom he assumed were the police on his back stairs.

"It's no use, Vasilov Bugàr," Mr. Smythe yelled into a police megaphone. "We have you surrounded."

Millicent couldn't believe her ears.

Bugàr? No, it couldn't be.

Was this the same villain who slipped through her fingers on her last assignment? The one who'd caused her to fail so miserably? Well, if that didn't just chap her shorts.

"Vasilov Bugàr." Millicent stepped out from behind Stillitano. "At last I now have a face to match your name. You . . . you . . . terrible person, you."

Stillitano rolled his eyes. He could think a host of obscenities to throw at the man who had nearly killed him, and who even now had his gun leveled at his head, but *you terrible person, you* wasn't one of them.

Nik jumped up onto his feet and circled the two captives. "You're correct, mademoiselle. I'm a terrible person, but through no fault of my own. I've come to avenge my family and my people the only way I can. Even if it means destroying one football player at a time."

Millicent gasped.

"No more funny business, Mr. Stillitano, or I will put a bullet from this gun in your head here and now."

Millicent knew she should probably be scared out of her skin, but for some reason she had the feeling that if she could stand up to this man, he might perhaps reconsider the odds of succeeding and give himself up to Mr. Smythe and Venetian police, who were also waiting for Bugàr to surrender.

"Don't listen to him, Mr. Stillitano," Millicent barked. "This man's nothing more than a bully, and the only way to deal with a bully is to refuse to cooperate with his demands."

Riccardo grimaced not knowing what exactly he should do next, but Millicent continued.

"Mr. Bugàr, I'm truly frustrated with your rash threats and aggressive behavior. You're obviously an intelligent man and can see your jig's about up. Besides, revenge taken out on innocent people is foolish at best and downright nasty at worse."

Riccardo grew more and more nervous as he watched Bugàr move in on the two of them. "Uh, signorina . . . ."

"Please be quiet, Mr. Stillitano. I have things totally in control." She turned her attention back to Bugàr. "Most of us, sir, have things we're trying to overcome, and you don't see us coming apart at the seams as a result. For example, I'm not clear as to who I am and what it is I'm doing here, but you don't see me acting childish and threatening to shoot blameless people."

"Are you about finished now, mademoiselle?" Bugàr hissed his words.

"The only thing I've left to say to you now, Mr. Bugàr, is shame on you."

What happened next transpired in a blur. As Mr. Smythe and three armed policemen in helmets, shields, and Kevlar vests burst into the room, Millicent gave a shriek.

"Mon Dieu!"

What the hell? French again?

In that brief nanosecond Stillitano momentarily broke his attention on Bugàr, only to have the evil man knock the footballer to the ground. At the same time Bugàr grabbed Millicent from behind in a choke hold and pressed the nose of his revolver against her temple.

Mr. Smythe spoke first. "Give yourself up, Bugàr, before you hurt someone else."

Bugàr gave a sinister laugh. "Like those former national football players who came into my village to rape our women and kill our men and boys? How many innocents were tortured and killed? And for what? A few laughs? A few gruesome stories to be told around the family table? No, I will never give up. Not until I've had my retribution on all those whose lives are even remotely connected to football!"

"You're a madman, Bugàr," Riccardo shouted from the floor.

"Shut up, you Italian clown." Bugàr wanted desperately to shoot the footballer, but he knew if he took his gun away from Millicent's head, he would immediately be shot dead.

Mr. Smythe, determined not to show Bugàr his concern for Millicent's life, spoke slowly and softly. "Please put down your gun, Bugàr, and let us talk this through. You haven't killed anyone yet, so think wisely about what you choose to do next."

"What I choose to do next is make my escape. And if you even dare to try and stop me, the woman you see in front of you will be no more."

"Eek!" Millicent squeaked.

Mr. Smythe had no other recourse but to motion his men to lower their weapons and back away from their target. Carefully Bugàr scuttled out the door and down the steps, dragging Millicent by the neck and using her as a shield. As soon as the two rounded the corner of the chapel, Mr. Smythe's men furtively descended the steps, careful to make sure Bugàr didn't see them following close behind.

Mr. Smythe momentarily stayed with Riccardo Stillitano until the emergency medical team arrived to check him out. Mr. Smythe had no doubt he and his men would eventually take Bugàr, but perhaps not before the madman took someone's life—like Millicent's, for example.

In the recent past whenever Millicent became hair-raisingly scared, she would either plummet silently into a full scale panic attack, or effervesce nonstop like the bubbles in a freshly uncorked bottle of prosecco. This occasion was of the second type. No matter how hard she tried, Millicent couldn't keep her mouth shut.

"Mr. Bugàr, I think it would be best for both of us if you would take Mr. Smythe's advice and let me go. You've made your so-called escape, and I will only slow you down should you leave this city. Of course, I've no idea as to where you think you can escape to. Mr. Smythe and his men have feelers all over the world. It is, after all, *international* football." The words

tumbled out of Millicent's mouth at the speed of light.

"And speaking of that, what do you have against football anyway, for

cat's sake? I'm sure whoever wronged you didn't do so because of football.

How silly is that? I mean, whoever heard of such a thing? I certainly

haven't."

Millicent let out one of her signature giggles.

"Tee-hee-hee."

"Don't you ever shut up, woman? You're driving me mad."

"Well, this isn't exactly pleasant for me either, you know. I've been

chloroformed, gagged, and tied to a chair, and then paraded through

Venice in my nightgown with a gun to my head. And now threatened with

my life. All I want to do is get my memory back—that's all. Dr. Martolini

has been very kind and helpful, but even he seems to be stymied by my

inability to remember who I once was, where I now am, and what I'm

doing at any given moment. You can't imagine what it's like to know you're

not yourself, and at the same time not remember who that self is?"

"For the love of Allah, shut up. Why I didn't shoot you in the basement

of the chapel when I had the chance, I'll never know."

Bugàr squinted his eyes as he focused ahead to make sure he was

seeing what he thought he was seeing—Luca waving at him from his

speedboat as it hugged the side of the narrow canal-way.

***

Alfredo ran as fast as he could, limited only by the young boy whose hand he held tightly. Holmes and Watson were also traveling as fast as their short legs and extended tongues allowed. Nothing in this moment was more important to the four of them than Millicent's safety.

At last they arrived at the chapel. Alfredo and Paolo followed the pugs around to the back stairs and watched the dogs hop up the steps one riser at a time. Not sure if they were flying into a trap or not, Alfredo held Paolo and himself back from moving up the stairs until he was sure the coast was clear. No sooner had Holmes and Watson disappeared into the apartment, but Mr. Smythe poked his head out of the doorway.

"I thought I told you to stay where you were." Mr. Smythe didn't sound as angry as he did resolute. "We have Stillitano, and according to the medical team here he appears to be all right. But we still don't have Bugàr in custody. Unfortunately, he craftily eluded our net, but my men are close on his trail."

Alfredo and Paolo flew up the stairs—Alfredo because he wanted to hold dear Millicent in his arms, and Paolo because Riccardo Stillitano was his favorite football hero.

"And Millicent? How is she?" Alfredo panted as he scanned inside the apartment for her.

Mr. Smythe put his arm around Alfredo's shoulders. "I'm sorry,

Alfredo. But I'm afraid she's with Bugàr. He used her as a hostage to ensure his escape, and we had no other recourse but to let him go."

"No, you can't let him have her. He will kill her, I'm sure of it." Alfredo wasn't the only one going crazy with fear. Holmes and Watson stopped dead in their tracks as well, before setting out to feverishly sniff the ground.

"Paolo, you stay here with the doctors and Signor Stillitano. I'm going to free Millicent if it's the last thing I do." Holmes and Watson had by now picked up Millicent's scent and were nosing their way down the back steps.

"Wait, Alfredo," interrupted Mr. Smythe. "I'm afraid I can't allow you to put yourself, Holmes and Watson, or my assistants in any more danger than you're already in. If you want to rescue Millicent and ensure her safety, I must go with you. But you'll have to do as I instruct. Do we understand each other?"

"*Sì, sì*. Let's go before we lose sight of the pugs. *Il mio piccolo carlini.*"

The two men hurried to keep up with Holmes and Watson. Alfredo was heard praying quietly under his breath, while at the same time Mr. Smythe spoke into his cell phone, coordinating efforts with his security people already in pursuit of Bugàr. Meanwhile, sitting on the edge of the bed inside the apartment, Riccardo Stillitano was being seen to by an emergency medical team of doctors, reassuring him that given time he would soon be fit enough to play football once again.

Paolo gingerly walked over to his idol. "Signor Stillitano," whispered

Paolo, "may I please have your autograph?"

Riccardo reached out for the boy and smilingly set him up onto his lap. "Of course, anything for the little man who has helped save my life."

***

Alfredo and Mr. Smythe had caught up to Holmes and Watson and only trailed them by a few yards. Ahead was what appeared to be a deserted canal.

Possibly wide enough for a shallow-hulled speedboat? Alfredo wondered as he felt his heart beat in anticipation.

"Not much further now, Alfredo," Mr. Smythe warned in a soft voice. "We must be very careful."

To the two men it seemed as though the canine detectives were about to turn a final corner, when suddenly out of nowhere appeared an oversized, mean-looking feral cat with a good one hundred or more feral cats at his side.

"Good God," Mr. Smythe exclaimed as he held his arm out to prevent Alfredo from advancing.

"*Mamma mia.* What are all these *gatti selvatici*, these wild cats, doing here? And why aren't Holmes and Watson breaking their ranks?" Alfredo asked between gasps.

"Shh. Quiet, Alfredo. We must trust Holmes and Watson to do what they know best."

210

Alfredo wiped his brow as he and Mr. Smythe watched the intense proceedings. Besides, all this running around was more exercise than Alfredo had experienced in years, and he honestly needed a few seconds to catch his breath.

Holmes and Watson were as surprised as the two men behind them at the sudden appearance of Morazzio and his fellow felines. They desperately wanted to barge through the snarl of cats, but thought better of it when they took in exactly how many had surrounded them. Instead they chose to stay where they were and take a moment to catch their breaths as well.

"So, we meet again. And for what do I owe this surprise visit, my *pugnacious* friends?" Morazzio laughed in spite of himself at his own pun. Noticing no one else was laughing, he abruptly stopped and eyed his minions with contempt. Then, they too, probably out of fear more than out of getting the joke, started laughing as well. Within seconds Morazzio turned his shrewd eyes onto Holmes and Watson.

"Ha. That's a good one, Morazzio," Holmes said, knowing full well the best thing to do with Morazzio was to go along with whatever he wanted. "'My pugnacious friends.' Very clever, Morazzio. Don't you think so Watson?"

"Yeah—'pugnacious friends'—clever," he snorted.

"Silence," Morazzio scowled. And immediately there was silence. "Answer my question, carlini."

Holmes took a few steps forward. "I know we are treading upon your territory once again, Signor Morazzio. And we are deeply sorry for that, but you must allow us to proceed for our dear Millicent has again found herself in a bit of a sticky wicket and needs our help in saving her life."

"Yeah, saving 'er life." Watson trotted up to stand shoulder to shoulder with Holmes.

"Not Millicent? What are you saying? What has happened?" In a flash Morazzio's face went from a threatening scowl to a terrified grimace. Holmes and Watson quickly described to the Don of the Venetian Feline Mafia all that had thus far transpired, only to watch the fat cat morph once again from scared witless to fiercely enraged. "Not only do you have my permission to continue tracking Millicent and that ass of a man, but you can rely on us to do what we can to bring him down."

Alfredo and Mr. Smythe watched the mystifying transaction with astonishment. "What do you think is going on?" Alfredo asked impatiently.

Mr. Smythe narrowed his eyes and took in the entire event detail by detail. "I'm not absolutely sure, but it looks to me like some sort of negotiation process is at hand."

"Of all the silly . . . ."

"Let's not be hasty, Alfredo. I've heard about this kind of thing before, and though I've never witnessed it for myself or held much truth in the idea that animals, particularly dogs and cats, can communicate with one

212

another, I'm having a change of heart."

Then, as quickly as they appeared, the retinue of feral cats vanished into the various nearby canals with their leader forging the way. Holmes and Watson continued toward the canal-way in front of them, barking instructions for Alfredo and Mr. Smythe to follow.

Chapter 16

"Mr. Bugàr, if you think I'm going to get me into that awaiting speedboat with you, you're gravely mistaken."

Up to that point Millicent had hoped Mr. Smythe and his men would've rescued her by now, but to her utter disappointment they were nowhere in sight. In fact, not a single living soul except a few canal cats parading up and down the promenade was available to hear her screams for help. Not Mr. Smythe, nor Holmes and Watson, nor . . .

"Alfredo, whah," Millicent sobbed.

"Ah, yes, *Doktor* Alfredo Martolini, that dirty double-crosser. Cry all your want, mademoiselle, but your dear Alfredo won't come to save you. No one will for only Luca and I know of this hidden canal," Bugàr snarled.

He was about to push Millicent into the waiting arms of Luca, when around the corner who should come but the two most precious beings in the world to Millicent—Holmes and Watson—and barking all the way.

Startled, Bugàr turned his attention toward the dogs.

Immediately Millicent snapped out of her self-pity and screamed at the top of her lungs. "Look out, boys. He's got a gun."

Bugàr raised his Makarov pistol at the dogs, but as soon as he did, Luca fired up the engines of his boat and sped off, leaving Bugàr no other recourse but to change his aim and fire upon his accomplice.

"*Srati*," Bugàr screamed. "*Srati, srati, srati!*"

Unfortunately for Bugàr but lucky for Luca the speedboat was already too far out of range for the bullets to do much if any damage. Bugàr then turned a complete one hundred and eighty degrees to now point his gun at Millicent. Instinctively, Millicent placed herself in front of Holmes and Watson who stood stock still behind her.

"This is your entire fault, Mademoiselle Whatever-Your-Name-Is. Yours and that of your stupid dogs."

Millicent's legs shook so profusely, the flower on her hat bounced from side to side in rapid succession. Her hiccups returned as well.

"Sir, this situation you find yourself in has very little if anything to do with me (*hiccup*) or my dogs, for that matter (*hiccup*). This has all been of your making from the day you kidnapped not only Mister (*hiccup*) Stillitano, but that goalkeeper from Atletico (*hiccup*) Madrid."

Bugàr gaped at Millicent in shock.

"Yes, I know all about your last endeavor (*ah-choo*), and even though you got away with taking the ransom money, I was the one who (*ah-choo*) made sure nothing further happened to that poor goalkeeper beyond your infantile skills of (*ah-choo*) torture."

Millicent hoped if she could at least keep Bugàr's attention a bit longer, Mr. Smythe and his men would surely show up.

"So, that was you, was it? I always wondered who was stupid enough to interfere with my plans, and now I know. Well, it won't happen again because now I have you right where I want you, down the sights of my gun barrel."

Bugàr cocked back the hammer of his revolver and was about to fire when he heard a familiar voice from behind him. "Put the gun down, Bugàr. No use trying to escape. My men have their rifles aimed at your head and are eager to fire upon my command."

Bugàr stood completely still. "Mr. Smythe. We meet again." Bugàr laughed brutally. "Now, you must of course realize I will never allow you to take me alive, yes? And if it's the last thing I do, my dying act will be to put this ridiculous woman out of all of our collective misery."

Alfredo was beside himself with fear. He wanted to run toward Millicent and whisk her away in his strong arms. Yet with Nik or Bugàr or Whatever-His Name holding a loaded gun, he knew the two of them probably wouldn't get far. Besides, Mr. Smythe had his arm outstretched, barricading Alfredo from the endangered Millicent.

"For the love of the blessed Virgin, Smythe, do something," Alfredo pleaded.

Millicent closed her eyes tight, hiccupped, and readied herself for the inevitable. That is, until she heard what sounded like a screaming banshee soar over her head and land where she imagined Bugàr to be standing.

She opened one eye.

And hiccupped. Followed by a sneeze.

"*Srati*. Shit. Get this beast off of me," Bugàr screamed frantically.

"What in the name of Heaven is that?" Alfredo exclaimed.

Mr. Smythe could do no more than laugh. "Now I've seen it all."

Seemingly from out of nowhere Morazzio had leapt onto the top of Bugàr's head and was ferociously clawing the criminal's face and scalp like the mafia don of the feral cats that he was. In an effort to pull his adversary off of his head, Bugàr dropped the Makarov. As soon as he did, hundreds of feral cats converged and overtook Bugàr, landing him in one fell swoop onto the ground.

Mr. Smythe's men had one hell of a time getting to Bugàr to save him from being totally shredded to pieces. Holmes and Watson were in on the action as well, barking and dancing about wildly.

While Mr. Smythe orchestrated Bugàr's arrest, handcuffs and all,

Alfredo ran to Millicent's side and took her in his arms. "Millicent, my darling, are you all right?"

Millicent felt her hat crumple against Alfredo's warm chest. Her glasses fogged up as well. Yet never had she felt so desirable in her life.

"I think so. However, I can't speak for my hat." She stared up into Alfredo's eyes and saw what she'd yearned to see for so long, *love.* He bent down, placed his mouth on her smiling lips, and kissed her for all he was worth. Millicent felt the electricity of his kiss zing through her eager body. As Alfredo lifted her in his arms from off the ground, her legs danced to the ecstasy surging through her heart. *Mon dieu!*

"All right, you two," Mr. Smythe said through a smile. "We need to get back to our midfielder and the boy to let them know we finally have Bugàr in custody. He won't be able to hurt anyone ever again. That is, at least not for a very long time."

Alfredo lowered Millicent's feet to the ground, not taking his eyes off of her for even a second. She smiled up at him, foggy glasses and all. "Does this mean you can no longer be my psychiatrist?"

Alfredo smiled back tenderly. "That's exactly what it means."

Holmes and Watson watched their two favorite people with big grins on both of their faces. Holmes gave a short bark to draw Millicent's attention. Watson mirrored his friend.

"I say, yip."

"Yeah, yip."

Millicent gazed down at her two closest friends who sat obediently at her feet. "Oh, and of course, my thanks to Holmes and Watson, and to you, Mr. Smythe, and to my new brave friend, Signor Morazzio," she said with a wink to the top cat.

A hundred and one cats meowed at once, Morazzio being the loudest.

Bugàr's scratched and bloodied face looked like a swollen eggplant. When his eyes at last met Millicent's, through swollen lips he spit out a final oath of vengeance. "You're going to be sorry for what you've done, mademoiselle. Sooner or later I'll have my revenge. And nothing will give me more pleasure than to watch you die at my own hands."

Hiccup.

Millicent and Alfredo watched as Mr. Smythe and his men took Bugàr away to be held overnight in a Venetian jail. Later Bugàr would be transported to Zurich, where he would stand trial for his crimes against football, specifically those involving the goalkeeper and the midfielder respectively. Yet before the special agents and their captive turned the corner and out of earshot, the two lovers heard Bugàr shout at them one last time.

"And you betrayed me as well, Alfredo. You told me you were my friend. Some friend, huh? I swear to you on the graves of my dead family, I will see you pay as well."

Morazzio sat back on his haunches, screeched at the villain, and showed him his sharp extended claws. "Yeeahhhooww!"

Holmes and Watson also took part by first sneezing in Bugàr's direction and then simultaneously lifting their legs to pee.

Millicent let out a sigh. "Well, I guess that about sums things up."

Alfredo smiled. "Sì, sì. You must know how very proud I am of you, Millicent. You've come a long way since we first met. You were so fragile then, I wasn't sure you would ever find your memory. But today you showed yourself to be a strong and courageous woman, well on her way to a full recovery."

Millicent frowned a bit. "You know, I still have terrible problems with my memory. And the visions I have are so vivid, they still appear to me as if they're real."

Alfredo hugged her closer. "I know my darling. You still have a way to go, but at long last I feel you're moving in the right direction."

"In more ways than one?" Millicent said flirtatiously.

"*Sì, la mia bellezza*, my beauty, in more ways than one." Millicent reached up to hold Alfredo's handsome face in her hands. And on tiptoe placed a kiss on Alfredo's lips, which she knew the two of them would never forget.

***

Millicent felt the October breeze blow through her long hair as she sat at the little café table enjoying her view of the Eiffel Tower. It was hard to believe it'd been less than a week since she enjoyed a cup of tea and a croissant seated on this same chair. The sun shone brightly for an autumn afternoon, but the breeze was cool enough to allow the hot tea to warm her.

She closed her eyes, savoring with piqued appreciation the sensorial splendor of this late afternoon. Soon she took in the aroma of a familiar Galois cigarette, and as she did, a subtle smile played upon her lips.

"Monsieur H, is it you?"

"Oui, mademoiselle, 'tis I, Inspector H of the Paris Sûreté at your service once again."

Millicent opened her eyes and smiled broadly at the short bald man with the sweet voice and demeanor. "I hoped you would find me."

"Ah, mademoiselle. I hoped to find you as well. I must say, you look somewhat different from when we were last seated here." He sat next to her, his hat in hand. "Have you done something different with yourself?"

"No, I don't think so. But thank you very much for the compliment all the same." Millicent blushed. "I feel different, that's for sure."

Inspector H took on a look of surprise. "Oh? In what way, may I ask?"

Millicent stirred the sugar which had settled in the bottom of her teacup. "It's difficult to explain, really. I feel much different from whom I once was, but still not truly myself, if that makes any sense."

The little man squinted his eyes in concentration. "Please, go on."

"Well, for one thing, often and apparently for no reason at all, I seem to be able to speak French fluently. I'm not French, I'm English—at least I think I am. And I'm fairly certain I've never ever been to France, except in my dreams, of course, like now, while I'm speaking with you."

"*Très intéressant.*" The Inspector blew his cigarette smoke into a set of perfect circles.

"Yes, I think so, too. *Moi aussi.* Oh dear. You see what I mean?"

Monsieur H listened carefully to Millicent, hesitant to give advice. The puzzlement of her mental malaise had to be pieced out by her and her alone, otherwise healing would perhaps never come. At least not to the depths of what would be needed for Millicent to recover fully and completely.

"*Oui, ma chérie.* And what about your memory lapses? Are you having any better luck in ascertaining when they occur and why?"

Oooh, he's good!

"Well, yes and no. I'm getting much better at remembering the visions I have when I either see things through the eyes of the criminal, or when I've my periodic visits from you. But I still struggle with huge segments of time where I feel as if I've left myself entirely. I mean, it's almost as if I suddenly become another person entirely."

"Ah, I see."

Millicent took another bite of the delicious croissant in front of her.

"But then just as quickly I return to myself and wonder where the hell I've been and what it was I'd been doing. On top of that, I talk to my dogs."

"That's not unusual, mademoiselle. Most people speak to their pets knowing full well they more than likely are not being understood."

"Yes, I know. But I have deep and profound conversations with Holmes and Watson—well, with Holmes anyway. Watson's a bit of a dolt."

Millicent sighed. "Honestly, I'm rather worried about myself."

Monsieur H took another drag off his Galois. "Have you spoken at any length about this with your psychiatrist, Doctor Martolini?"

Millicent hesitated, popped the rest of the croissant in her mouth, and gulped down the last swallow of tea remaining in her teacup. "Well, there's a problem now with that."

"Oui?"

"Oui, Alfredo no longer is my doctor—he's my, uh . . . ." Millicent glanced down at her hands. "Well, I'm not quite sure what he is as of yet, but I don't think I'll be consulting him about my memory issues in the near future." She raised her smiling face and looked her mentor directly in the eyes. "If you know what I mean." And then she winked.

***

Nether Wallop, England

Millicent had arrived home the day after Bugàr's arrest and slept for three days straight. Aunt Kate still hadn't returned to the UK, so Millicent got out of bed from time to time to feed the boys or to let them outside to do their business. Alfredo also called a time or two to see how she was doing. And to make sure Millicent knew he was doing everything in his power to reschedule his many clients in order to spend time with her at her home in Nether Wallop.

She hadn't seen Alfredo since the day they stood together on the canal-way in Venice, exchanging hugs and kisses. And oh, how she missed him.

As of yet she still hadn't heard from Mr. Smythe, which was probably a good thing for she was in no shape whatsoever to take on another case—not yet anyway.

But she did remember her dream of meeting Inspector H at the familiar sidewalk café in Paris. In fact, with each visit from her friend and mentor she was able to recall more and more detail. The taste of the croissant, the warmth of the tea, the breeze blowing through her long hair, and, of course, the smell of the smoke from those ghastly Galois cigarettes.

She even recollected important moments like cruising down the Seine on an open-decked riverboat, dancing the tango at a *milonga* in Buenos Aires, and gliding through the ancient canals of Venice in an artfully crafted black patinated gondola.

During their last telephone conversation Alfredo promised he would arrive at Millicent's sometime later that day. All he had to do was make sure his mamma was taken care of and not miss his flight out of the Marco Polo airport. His sister, Cecilia, and her husband, Gino, lived in the countryside outside of Venice and had invited the elder Signora Martolini to stay at their home for the week or at least until Alfredo returned.

The flight from Venice to London would take the better part of two hours. Upon arrival Alfredo would then need to rent a car and drive forty minutes or so south to Nether Wallop.

The collywobbles in Millicent's stomach hadn't stopped since she'd gotten out of bed that morning. It'd been a long time since she'd made love with a man. That is, she thought it'd been some length of time, but, of course, she wasn't completely sure.

In any case, she straightened her house, picked up after the dogs, took a long bubble bath, and put on enough makeup to accent her blue contact-lensed eyes. The clothes she'd worn in Venice were torn and dirty, so she searched her closet for something she hoped Alfredo would appreciate.

"Holmes. Watson. Come here and help me pick out a dress. I want to make sure I look my best when Alfredo arrives."

The two pugs trotted into Millicent's bedroom and watched as she pulled several items from her closet for their approval. Earlier they'd dressed in the new outfits Millicent had purchased during her stay in Venice. Holmes sported his new red and white plaid hat and matching sweater vest, and Watson his new red bowtie and white tails. They appeared as if they were to serve as Grand Marshals for the festival boat regalia held each summer along the Grand Canal of Venice.

Millicent slipped on her favorite midnight blue silk dress. She decided a pair of silk stockings and gold strappy high heels would best bring out the classical lines of the gown. She then dug out her twenty-one karat gold necklace with matching earrings she'd kept hidden in her jewelry box for the last three years, waiting for an occasion such as this to unveil them.

She brushed her hair one last time before spraying on her favorite perfume. As she heard the rental car pull up, she quickly painted her lips red to match Holmes's and Watson's outfits. Her heart pounded so hard within her chest that for a moment she thought she would pass out.

The doorbell rang.

With Holmes and Watson seated at her feet, Millicent stood but a few feet from the door, knowing what lay on the other side could very well be her destiny. She took in a deep breath and then with a smile on her face, she opened the door to what she hoped were Alfredo's waiting arms.

"*Bon jour,* Alfredo."

The handsome doctor stood frozen before her, a look of shock on his face.

"Veronica, I mean Millicent, I mean . . . What are you doing here? *Mamma mia,* is it really you?"

The **Millicent Winthrop** Series

Thank you for being a fan of Gwen Overland! Please feel free to head to Amazon and leave a book review. Every review received means the world to independent authors.

To stay on top of all mystery and mayhem in the Millicent tales, go to **cunigundavalentine.com** to see exclusive content, win prizes, and sign up for our newsletter!

For a read that's a bit *Hotter*...

The *Hot in* HAWAII Series

What happens when four ruggedly sexy cowboys living on separate Hawaiian islands become entangled with the women that will eventually lasso their hearts? The bronco-busting ride to romance for each of these four couples is wrought with hesitations, complications, secrets, half-truths, and lies, but in the end, they discover that it's more than the weather that's *Hot in Hawaii*.

1 - Kona Cowboy Surfer

2 - Oahu Cowboy SEAL

3 - Kaui Cowboy Senator

4 - Maui Cowboy Surgeon

To learn more about the sexy cowboys of Hawaii and their relationship turmoil, go to **gwenoverland.com/hotinhawaii**, and sign up for our newsletter!

After years in academia, writing one research article followed by another, Gwen turned her talents toward writing fiction and found she happily could not stop.

In addition to writing cozy mysteries under her pseudonym **Cunigunda Valentine**, Gwen also writes romance novels and has published non-fiction books on the work she does in conjunction with her business, **Expressive Voice Dynamics**.

She currently lives in Ashland, Oregon, home of the Oregon Shakespeare Festival, with her family and her beloved black pug. Prior to that, Gwen lived in Los Angeles and had careers in directing, acting, and singing while performing at the piano. She's a Puget Sound gal at heart though, and you'll catch glimpses of this beautiful Washington area sprinkled throughout some of her books.

Made in the USA
Middletown, DE
14 July 2024

57266312R00130